DREW AND THE DETECTIVES

THE
RHYTHM
OF *BETRAYAL*

ANDREW PACHOLYK
MS, L.Ac
INTERNATIONAL BEST SELLING AUTHOR
author of *Barefoot: A Surfer's View of the Universe*

The Rhythm of Betrayal
by Andrew Pacholyk MS L.Ac
Copyright © 2024

Editor: Angela Mikaela
Book Cover Design and Interior Formatting by 100Covers.

ISBN   978-1-7353199-7-1 (paperback)
        978-1-7353199-6-4 (ebook)
Library of Congress Control Number: 2024904663
Know Publishing, New York, NY

DEDICATION

To my gypsy family, *te amo*. "I've learned if you want to empower
yourself, spend time with people you respect and admire,
who live their truth."

Debra Arditi
Deborah Desilets
Israel Loreto Diaz
Vincent Dixon
Lani Ford
Francesca Muia
Aisha Qandisha
Grace Redwood
Kyle Rizeq

CONTENTS

CHAPTER 1
OCEAN DRIVE

THE LOW ROAR of an engine could be heard revving in the distance. It was only 10am in the morning, yet the searing Miami sun was already melting the rubber handle bars on Debra's red and white Schwinn bicycle as she and Drew raced down the middle of Ocean Drive, enjoying the early morning lack-of-traffic. The pristine, art-deco hotels lined the beachfront boulevard like guardians from a divine era. The smell of salty air lilted across the beach like an aromatic invitation to a carefree life. It wasn't until they hit 4th street that Drew and Debra realized they were being targeted by the maniac in the black sports car with tinted windows. Its missing hood ornament was a testament to its already ominous nature.

The car ripped past them, just missing Debra by an inch! The bold, Argentinian heiress quickly spun her cycle around to stop and curse out the driver.

"My God, are you alright?" Drew yelled, in shock.

"This idiot must be drunk," she snapped back, her legs straddling the bike in a defiant stance as she checked to see if she was in one piece.

Before they knew it, the death machine had spun around and was now facing them. The driver revved the engine, as a bull would huff and sneer right before it would attack. The car hit the gas. The wheels spun faster

1

as the vehicle exploded towards them, barreling down Ocean Drive in the wrong direction.

"He's comin' for us," Drew exclaimed, giving Debra the warning.

Without hesitation, she pivoted the bike and peddled for her life. "We should split up," she screamed to Drew.

Now, the black mystery car raced toward his target, and that bullseye was Debra. The smell of tar and burnt rubber preceded them as the crazed driver attempted to level the blond beauty in seconds flat.

Drew popped his front wheel forward, taking him halfway up the stairs of the neighboring coffeeshop. The move got him out of the direction of the mad killer as he turned his wheels to see where Debra was.

She was now midline to the car's grill, only four feet away from what was sure to be a devastating end. But the agile dancer was as proficient on the dance floor as she was on her two-wheeler. She spotted a ramp in between the medium, dividing the two-way street. She launched her bike skyward, sailing into the opposite lane just as the black metallic demon missed her by inches. She crossed over onto the sidewalk and kept headed straight for the beach.

There was nothing the maniac could do now. Drew watched as the death car came to a screeching halt. It idled for what seemed like a minute, the assassin, perplexed, then sped off in the opposite direction. The ominous image was now seared in Drew's brain.

He stood there trying to catch his breath. Sweat dripping down his taut body. He was still in amazing shape even in his early 40s. No doubt, his years as a professional dancer and surfer preserved his frame. His analytical mind attempted to make sense of the events of the last few moments.

"What, did you guys stop for coffee?" Francesca, aka Francy, came wheeling around the corner on her 10-speed bike. "We were looking everywhere for you two."

Francy was an incredible dance teacher with the body of a fitness model to match. A slight remanence of an Italian accent was still evident even with her street-smart attitude. She slid her bike up towards Drew, with youthful abandon, using her powerful legs to stop the cycle right on point.

Tailing behind her was Spain's version of Brigitte Bardot. Propped up on her rental bike, Aisha raced up with her hands in the air. "Que pasa?" Her sweat glistened on her perfectly groomed body, as she stopped to pull back her golden hair into a ponytail.

As his two friends listened intently, Drew quickly tried to explain the terrorizing attempt on their lives.

"Where's Debra?" Aisha asked, not quit comprehending what was happening.

"Here I am!" Debra pulled up behind the group, clearly frustrated, wondering why she was the intended target.

"Are you alright?" Francy asked with serious concern.

Drew intervened. "Look at her. Anyone else would be in shock or hysterical, but not Debra. Our feisty and resilient girl is not going to let drama like this ruffle her aura."

Debra was already trying to figure out what was going on. "I'm fine. I want to know who that crazed lunatic was."

"Did you see the driver?" Francy asked, pulling her dark brunette hair back into a ponytail.

"Or get a license plate?" Aisha echoed.

As in sync, Drew and Debra both answered. "The windows were tinted over, and the license plate was missing. It even looked like someone bit off the hood ornament."

"He was probably some drunk dude, left over from last night, looking for trouble. Well, we better get to dance," Francy suggested. "I can't be late to my own class."

Arriving at the gym just minutes before, they were met by a young guy on a skateboard, racing to make sure he wouldn't be late.

"Hey, Israel," Drew announced, "you missed all the excitement already. Debra and I were being chased by a mad man."

The always joking, 20-something quickly retorted, "You should see who I was chasing this afternoon?" he said with a devilish grin. Dressed in a tank top and jean shorts, he whisked his short chestnut hair back and came to a quick stop on his skateboard.

Francy and Aisha quickly recapped the mayhem that Debra and Drew went through to Israel. "It's a good thing those two are quick on their feet," Israel reassured them. "Otherwise, we'd be scrapping them off Ocean Drive."

Drew spotted the other two dancers from his close-knit group of friends and caught up with them. Grace and Elena were coming up the steps to the gym when Drew reached them. His heart was still racing as he told them what had happened.

Grace, a glowing African beauty was a warm, easy-going girl in her mid-30s yet she imbued a motherly personality twice her age. Always making sure everyone was taken care of. "I don't know what I would have done." Grace said, grasping her heart.

She was complimented by her good friend, Elena, a New York musician and singer. Savvy with a typical New York edge, she and Drew had been friends from the entertainment circuit for years. She was dressed in form fitting dance wear with her hair in pigtails, a look juxtaposed to her dry sense of humor. "Are you sure Debra wasn't chasing him?"

Grace approached Debra with a cautious step. She saw the fear in her eyes and recognized it well, but she couldn't let Debra crumble. Not now. "Girl, are you doing, ok?" she said softly, placing her hand on Debra's shoulder.

Debra looked up at her friend, desperate for solace. "I can't stop thinking about what happened," she cried.

"I know, but you have to stay strong," Grace urged. "What can we do? How can we help?" Grace had a special way of calming the spirit. Her empathic nature gave her an authoritative strength.

Debra tried to swallow down the anxiety rising in her throat. She didn't like being coddled. She thought it made her appear weak. "I just need to keep my mind busy."

"Okay, that's good. We'll dance off the stress," Grace said encouragingly. She pulling her long green braids back behind her, wrapping them into a tight knot.

As they entered the 1,500 square foot dance studio, it gleamed with warm Miami Beach sunlight streaming through its floor to ceiling windows on the north and eastern sides. A wall of mirrors faced the dancers while large glass windows on the west end faced outwards towards the gym for all to see.

"You see Debra, you have plenty of space to breathe here," Elena commented with her New York accent. She encouraged Debra to take a deep breath.

The room was well vented. Above their heads were sound proof barrier panels strategically placed to hide the vaulted ceilings and the spaces between. The ceiling was strung with hammocks for ariel yoga, long silver poles for pole dance classes, and ballet barres that extended downwards. Its specially designed hardwood floors were crafted for comfort. It was the place where all the magic happened.

This "click of seven" were thick as thieves. Although they were from a variety of cultural backgrounds, ages, and races, this unlikely group of friends were all very close. And what was the glue that bound them together?

Dance. They all shared a common belief. "We are most alive when we're dancing," Francy would always say. "Even though we are from different schools and possess a variety of unique techniques, we make magic when we dance."

Francy was the one who united all her students for that one hour of pride and joy. Dance was the one language all her students understood, and they understood it very well. She could command as many as 30 students in class.

Once the music started, the class was hypnotized. Their minds engaged in the movement, while they interpreted the intricate nuances of the music. People would stop to watch the dancers through the studio windows facing the gym. Transfixed at their synchronicity and flow of motion, gym members would breakout in applause when they finished a dance.

Drew found his tribe. Along with Grace, Elena, Israel, Debra, and Aisha, Francy found six friends who thought alike. They would perform in Miami's hottest nightclubs, hotels, and events. Dubbed the "Sexy Seven" by Miami's hyperbolic press, these dancers were so in-tune with each other that it felt like they were all part of a single, unified organism.

If only life could be that succinct.

When the class ended, the routine of coming down off that high took some time. The dancers lingered in the room recovering from the workout.

Israel walked over to Debra, as he dried the sweat from his forehead. He whisked his towel around his neck. "What are your plans for tonight?"

"I have a date with Ansel White," Debra replied weakly.

Grace raised her eyebrows in surprise. "The shipping tycoon? I heard he has a twin brother?"

Before Debra could answer, Elena came running over. "Who has a twin brother? I saw him first." she laughed breathlessly.

"Ansel White!" Grace exclaimed. "You know, the Miami shipping heir?"

Elena's face turned somber as she spoke. "Grace, did you hear? Ansel's father passed away under horrible circumstances this week--a cargo crate fell on him at the docks," she said twirling her pigtails nervously.

"I heard that. Why would a man his age even be there so late at night?" Grace wondered aloud.

They looked to Debra for an answer, but all they could do was watch her as she stared silently at her reflection in the mirror, lost in thought. The girls pondered the strange circumstances surrounding Ansel White's father.

"OH, enough of this aimless thinking," Debra cried. "Drew? Let's go. This bunch is driving me crazy."

Drew ran over from his conversation with Aisha and Francy. "How did you get through that class?"

"You're babying me too? You just went through the same thing I did."

Drew gave Elena a knowing look as he changed the subject. "Where is Ansel taking you tonight?

"He wouldn't say," Debra frowned. 'It's some big surprise."

"Well, I have a singing gig tonight, Elena offered. "It's on some cruise ship."

"Francy, Aisha, and I are booked for a samba gig this evening," Grace volunteered. "Aisha has the details."

The girls had a side hustle dancing in Vegas showgirl-style costumes in restaurants and big events such as weddings and birthdays.

"I'm amazed that you girls have time for that, even with all the nightclub jobs we dance in," Debra tweeted as she grabbed Drew's arm and strutted out of the dance studio.

"Hey, wait up," Israel shouted.

Drew and Debra turned around to see their friend Israel's skateboard approach, wheels clattering against the pavement and flying up over the curb outside the gym. His perfect dismount landed him directly in front of them. Israel always seemed to have a happy-go-lucky attitude about him. He appeared to follow life in the direction the wind blew that day, positively and with confidence.

"Did you see that crowd today? They loved us." Israel was referring to the gym members applauding their dance performance. "Did you see 'la jaguar'?"

"Who? Katie Roma? She insists I go to some party tonight," Drew said, his brow furrowed with hesitation. "Did you call Katie a jaguar?" Drew laughed. "That's fitting."

"Katie Roma is Ansel's sister's girlfriend," Debra scoffed, rolling her eyes skyward in disbelief. "How can you be friends with her? She's so two-faced."

"She's always been nice to me," Drew replied with a shrug and a smile.

"Well, I don't trust her," Debra retorted.

"I don't know her," Israel laughed. "But she loves how we dance!"

"What are you doing tonight, Israel?" Drew asked as they meandered down Washington Avenue.

"I have a bartending job tonight."

Debra reached for the handle of her BMW doors and with a click, they unlocked. "Anyone need a ride?" she offered.

"Where's your bike?" Israel asked.

"In my trunk. The front fender got misaligned during a car chase with a maniac on Ocean Drive earlier this morning," Debra scoffed, sarcastically.

The three went their separate ways.

Drew kept looking over his shoulder on his bike ride home. What was the significance of that terrible attack?

Why did it seem like they were after Debra? Maybe that maniac thought she would be the easier target. But why? Was it a hate crime? Or just a crazy drunk on a joy ride?

As Drew entered his apartment, he was greeted by the gleaming mid-day sun that poured through the large windows. The spacious living room was a vibrant white, except for a pop of celestial blue linen curtains stretching from floor to ceiling, dancing to the warm tropical breeze. The simplicity offered a lively ambiance that was both expansive and austere. For Drew, it was a long way from New York, but it brought him peace.

There was an array of awards and photographs that adorned one wall strategically placed to glisten in the afternoon glow. Each accolade served as a reminder of his successful past, a testament to the hard work and dedication that had brought him here.

He sprawled out on the large white leather sofa and let out a long, deep exhale. He gazed up at the bookshelf. It was filled with numerous psychology books, from classics like Freud to contemporary authors like Kahneman. He often spent his free time devouring these books, seeking insights into the human mind and the factors that influenced decision-making.

His one-track mind circled back to the psychotic driver that chased him and Debra down Ocean Drive. The reality was just now seeping deep into his psyche. Why did that happen? It continued to haunt him.

His fascination with psychology, body language, and people's emotional responses fueled his relentless pursuit of understanding the complexities of human behavior. Drew's inquisitive nature compelled him to delve deep into the intricacies of human thought, aiming to unravel the mysteries that lie beneath people's actions and choices.

He turned on some music. " Oh, I love this song," he told himself.

His feet pulled together as he jumped up in one explosive movement from the sofa and started to salsa across the floor. His muscular frame moved effortlessly to the infectious beat as he danced around the living room.

Drew's passion for dance was a testament to his discipline and drive. But, according to society, dancers had a shelf-life. The span of a dancer's career was short-lived. Like any athlete, they had an expiration date. It's a good thing Drew didn't believe that. Of course, he didn't miss pounding the streets of New York for auditions, working part-time gigs between dance jobs, or starting life all over again every time a show closed. He did miss the comradery. That's when he found his new family of dancers in Miami.

"Oh no," he realized as the song finished, "I've got to get ready. I'm gonna be late!"

CHAPTER 2

BAYSIDE

THE UBER DRIVER pulled up and pointed to a shimmering stretch of waterfront in the distance. "Bayfront Park," he said with a nod. "You can find the private docks near the east end. Just follow the water."

In the night sky above, the full moon hung low, illuminating the sea with its radiant amber light. Drew stepped out of the car, dressed in beige linen pants and a royal blue linen shirt that made his sun-streaked blond hair pop against the evening glow. He stepped with purpose towards the glittering horizon, his polished shoes reflecting each ray of moonlight.

As he got closer to the waterfront his gaze drifted upward to a name etched in golden letters: The Kiss of the Sea. This mammoth yacht loomed up from the water like something out of a dream, draped in lights and accessorized with an immense number of beautiful people. Attired in their silky dresses and slick suits, the Miami elite popped like spring flowers against the gleaming white surface.

At its plank stood a young woman in a sailor's uniform. "Welcome to the funeral of Captain Falcon White," she offered.

Drew's smile disappeared. "I'm sorry, I must have the wrong boat," Drew addressed the young girl.

Glimpsing the invitation, she confirmed, "You're in the right place."

Now, completely perplexed by what he was doing, Drew mounted the impressive watercraft as a waiter handed him a flute of champagne on his way across the bow. He passed through the lobby and into an enormous room crowned with a domed atrium, which contained a line of palm trees in pots running down the center of the circular platform. The impressive yacht was iridescent from top to bottom dressed in bunting for the celebration and holding court amongst the tiny boats nearby.

"You've arrived," Katie Roma announced, grabbing Drew's arm as she slinked up behind him. Two air kisses and a hug followed.

"Katie, what is this? A funeral?" Drew whispered.

She could sense his uneasiness. "Oh honey, relax. It's not a funeral. But it is a send-off of sorts," Katie returned. "The entire White family is glad he's gone, so it's a celebration."

Dripping in a white flowing Calvin Klein floor-length dress, Katie's long brunette locks were pulled back by two diamond studded barrettes. Drew laughed to himself, remembering Israel's nickname for her.

"Katie, my love," a shrilled voice called out from behind them. Ansel's sister, Daphne White, the youngest of the three White siblings, smiled warmly as she approached her girlfriend. She draped her arm around Katie's shoulder. "There you are."

Katie gestured toward Drew, who stood nervously beside them. "This is my friend, Drew from that fierce dance group at the gym I told you about."

Daphne held out her hand to be kissed. Drew obliged. There was a moment of awkward silence before Daphne asked rhetorically, "Did you know my father?"

"I knew of him," Drew said quickly, a hint of apprehension in his voice.

"Well, it's just as well. He was a bitter old man," Daphne replied casually.

Drew quickly tried changing the subject. "I smell a beautiful fragrance. Is that rose?"

"You have a good nose," Katie reacted. "It's a delicate scent Daphne brings me that is only found in Saudi Arabia. Taif Rose," she smiled. "It's intoxicating."

"It's my favorite," Daphne chimed in.

"Drew," a familiar voice sang out. "You're here."

"That seems to be the general consensus," he replied, spinning around to find Debra draped over Ansel White's arm.

"Ansel White," he said, introducing himself to Drew, as they shook hands. The tall and distinguished looking Navy man was dressed in full uniform. He gleamed an impressive smile, as he squeezed Debra's arm tighter, drawing her into him.

"Brother, where is that obnoxious twin of yours," Daphne drilled.

Ansel ignored her.

The three White children were constantly battling each other, which made for great fodder for the gossip columns. Scrutinized by Miami's press and social media, Daphne was usually pegged as the one who wore a permanent scowl, her words usually dripping with sarcasm. Ansel was the golden boy who spoke in an even tone, poised and dignified, and carrying himself with authority. While Walter, the twin brother to Ansel, was often overlooked or seen as an afterthought.

"You must see the view from the top deck," Daphne announced. The group made their way through the crowd, winding the spiral staircase to the upper deck of the massive yacht.

Bayfront Park spanned over 32 acres of downtown Miami's stunning cityscape, glimmering like precious jewels catching the light. "I love it here," Katie Roma whispered to Drew.

"You should," Drew smiled. "It's your port."

Katie was the port director and CEO of Miami Moves. The world's leading hub for global shipping.

The sound of a familiar voice serenading the yacht's state-of-the-art acoustics filled the air. Debra and Drew looked at each other with surprise. "Elena!" they shouted in unison. Turning, they saw their friend with a microphone in her hand, singing on the far side of the boat. She was wearing a canary yellow dress with a scarf draped over her slender neck. She gave them both an acknowledging nod.

"Ansel, when are you dumping dad's ashes over the side?" Daphne insisted.

"What do you care, sis?" Ansel smiled in a calm demeanor.

"I don't," she replied. "I was just making pleasant conversation."

Debra leaned into Ansel, "My dear, are you really going to do that?"

He smiled and simply patted her hand. Ansel was a distinguished 60s-something, 25 years her senior, but Debra liked mature men. Being rich didn't hurt. His navel uniform was a glimpse into his disciplined life and his mannerisms matched that of a confident and handsome leader.

Suddenly, there was loud crash, which sounded like glasses hitting the floor. The group turned to see Israel dressed in a black tuxedo holding what was left of a tray full of champagne glasses and Walter White running away from him. "Make a hole!"

"Israel," Debra screamed in shock, "of course it's you in the middle of this."

Israel shrugged his shoulders as Walter, Ansel's disheveled twin brother dashed to the edge of the boat and vomited over the side.

"Walter, it serves you right," Daphne reacted. She turned to the group, "He started drinking 48 hours ago. What do you expect?"

Walter gained his composure, wiped the remaining remnants from his face and stumbled over to Daphne. "Good evening family," he mumbled.

"Walter, you're two sheets to the wind," Ansel commented, shaking his head.

"Walter, what's wrong with you?" Daphne reprimanded him. "All the guests are staring."

"Flotsam and jetsam," Walter managed. "All the guests, sis? All the guests are not up here."

Ansel turned and whispered in Debra's ear. "It means information or things of no real value. Navy talk."

"I was wondering what he was trying to say," Debra confirmed.

Walter appeared the exact opposite of his twin brother. Dressed in a 1970s beige leisure suit, his posture and demeanor were that of a much older man. He was out of shape and appeared to have a limp. Ansel turned to Debra and suggested they go below deck. As they walked away, Walter commented, "You can't go far on a moving boat."

"The boat is docked, you idiot." Daphne shook her head walking away with Katie arm in arm.

Drew made his way over to assist Israel. "Dude, are you alright?"

"Oh ya," he answered. "This guy plowed right over me trying to get to the side of the boat so he wouldn't heave all over the place."

"I didn't know this was your bartending job," Drew said helping him pick up the broken shards of glass.

"Me either. I just had a phone message giving me the time and address for work. I figured it was my agency. They are usually short on details. Hey, is this yours?" Israel bent down and picked up a flash drive that was laying among the pieces of champagne glasses.

"Let me see that," Drew said observing the metal stick with a white lightning streak on a red background along the side.

A hand reached up and touched Drew's shoulder. He jumped in fright. He quickly tossed the flash drive back to Israel, who slipped it into his pants pocket and turned around.

"I don't usually have that effect on men," Elena smiled.

"Geez. You scared the life right out of me." Drew confessed.

"Not enough, apparently. You're still standing," Elena laughed, raising one eyebrow.

"Hey, nice vocal set. You were fantastic," Israel complimented Elena.

"This is some funeral. I hope mine is as festive," she said. The three of them looked around as the party was in full swing. Loud bouts of laughter were shared with revelers dancing as the music started building. Like the fizz in a champagne bottle, the anticipation was palpable.

The boys cleaned up the mess and the three friends made their way over to the bar. "Thanks for helping me. Let me buy you a drink," Israel offered. He prepared them two mojitos.

"I'll have another champagne," Elena commanded. "Cheers! To the crazy Miami life."

"Everyone that's come up to the bar for a drink has been talking about the death of the tycoon," Israel whispered. "They say Falcon White was murdered." He tossed a bar rag over his shoulder, as he poured another guest some wine.

"Oh, he was. And I have a good idea who did it."

Drew looked at the girl Israel was pouring wine for. He recognized the sailor's uniform. "Hi, we meet at the gang plank," Drew introduced himself.

"Lizette Brown. I am..." she cleared her throat. "I was Captain Falcon White's personal assistant."

"Ohhh, I'm so sorry for your loss," Israel reacted, not knowing what to say next.

Drew's face changed. "I thought the news said it was an accident?"

The detective on the case told me to keep my theories to a minimum," Lizette frowned. "He said we need evidence."

"Some think it was the son, Walter," Israel leaned in to share his secret.

"Oh, you mean the guy who just bowled you over?"

Israel's face turned pale. "That was Walter White?" Israel choked on his mojito.

"In the flesh," Drew responded.

"They are saying he lured his father out to the docks that night and dropped a shipping crate on his head." Israel was now visibly shaking.

"Well, you should know... this family is crazy." Lizette gulped down her wine and left the group with a parting shot. "Just watch your backs," she turned and darted for the lower deck.

"How is it that we all ended up here tonight?" Elena pondered as she knocked back another glass of bubbly.

"Well, not all of us," Drew offered.

"That's what you think," Israel laughed looking past the bar to the spiral staircase. The music changed. The room exploded with feathers and colorful balloons as six stunning samba dancers descended the staircase. Dripping in colorful plumage, sparkling costumes, and tall headdresses, the dancers were followed by three rhythmic drummers. The drums engaged their gyrating bodies in a fiery and enticing dance around the ship, led by none other than Francy.

Grace and Aisha shimmied by their friends, screaming in joy as the trio was just as surprised to see them dancing across the ballroom floor.

"There is something fishy going on?" Elena suggested, now two sheets to the wind. "Why are we all here and none of us knew it?"

Israel and Drew looked at each other, wondering. Was it the alcohol talking, or did she have a point?

Israel brushed it off to coincidence. "Well, Miami's essentially a small town."

"Debra should be here to see the girls dancing," Elena slurred.

"She is." Israel pointed to a corner of the yacht were Debra and Ansel were cozying up to each other.

"You're too observant for your own good," Drew pointed out. "She's not paying attention anyway."

Debra started waving her arms frantically in the direction of her friends, pointing to the top of the stairs.

Francy and Aisha were back at the top of the staircase. The crowd erupted in raucous applause as Joyce White, the widow of the late Captain Falcon White accompanied the dancers.

A short, powerhouse of a woman with jet black hair and pearlescent skin, she gleamed a brilliant smile as she shimmied down the staircase side by side with Francy and Aisha.

The male crew from the boat were at the bottom of the staircase to meet her. They joined her in the samba and the guests went wild! They escorted her right up to the microphone as she took her gracious bow. The crowd applauded her grand entrance.

"Welcome everyone," Joyce White announced. "Thank you for being a part of Falcon's life celebration. He would have been proud to see you all gathered here," she smiled. "Our children - Ansel, Daphne, Walter and I wish to thank you from the bottom of our hearts."

Debra, who slinked up behind Drew, leaned in close to him, her voice barely a whisper, "So sincere," she said sarcastically.

Elena and Israel quickly turned to acknowledge Debra's presence.

Before Drew could comment, Elena gasped loudly as Debra held up her left hand to show off the glistening 4-carat engagement ring.

"You're engaged?!" he stammered.

"Can you believe it? Look at this ring!" Debra replied excitedly.

Elena grasped Debra's hand and stared cross-eyed into the reflective diamonds. "How sobering," she cooed.

"Congratulations sweetheart," Israel beamed.

"There. At least someone is happy for me." Debra confirmed.

"Hey bar boy, I need some drinks." The group was interrupted by a tall, dark and handsome Latin man dressed in tight form fitting pants and a black spandex top that displayed every bit of his worked-out body.

"Yo, let me get two Bellini's," he said to Israel.

"Yes please," Elena purred. "Who is that?"

Debra leaned in and whispered, "Castro Pryorr. He's a trainer at the gym."

"He should be my trainer," Elena confirmed.

"Ditto," echoed Israel.

"Too late!" Grace and Aisha had finished their performance and joined their friends at the bar. They were adorned in beautiful dresses with their after-performance glow. "He's got a squeeze," Grace confirmed.

The group watched the sexy trainer cross the room and hand a drink to Joyce White as he planted a long and lingering kiss on her lips.

"Mama has no shame," Aisha admitted.

"And at her husband's funeral." Grace was in shock, along with most of the group.

"This has been rumored to be going on long before his death, mi amor," Debra confirmed. "Ansel has been furious about his mother's behavior... and especially in public."

Aisha tapped Drew on the shoulder. "Look..." He turned and noticed the disturbance near the stage.

"Ex, excuse, excuse me everybody," a staggering male voice growled over the loudspeaker. "I want your... attention."

The DJ lowered the music as he watched Walter White stumble up to the stage and pull the microphone out of its stand. "This is my father's funeral. He, he, he... was a tortured man." Walter's drunken state, withstanding, his posture suddenly changed. Walter straightened his back, found his resolve, and cleared his throat loudly. He leaned into the microphone again. "Falcon White was murdered and one of you is the killer!"

CHAPTER 3

DOWNTOWN

MIAMI HAD A reputation for incredible nightlife and the city always had evenings filled with excitement. The following night was no different. This night, the Penta-glam Club, Miami's hottest mega complex was hosting Miami's hottest dance group.

A heavy silence filled the nightclub, like a clear lake with no wind. A single conga drum started the rhythm. 16 beats per measure. A rhythmic duo of drums joined in creating a trio.

The partiers waited on edge, anticipating the next note. An ethereal piano rippled over the driving beat of the percussion. Everyone inhaled... It proved a delicate balance between expectation and release.

"The crowd is antsy," Drew thought to himself. "They haven't made a sound, but I can feel them waiting for the bass." Debra nudges him with excitement.

Another deep breath... The bass dropped! All hell broke loose. The crowd screamed and rocked back and forth, now in anticipation of what was to follow. They knew this song and they already loved it. Their bodies intuit how to move perfectly with the rhythm -- feet stomping, hands clapping high above their heads. Now the undulating crowd was in sync, twitching bodies ready for climax. The DJ laced a familiar song over the drumbeat; everyone was waiting for the words to drop like bombs that would explode them into pieces.

The lyrics dropped. The crowd went mad. Drew and his dance friends, who were huddled on stage left, hidden in the dim light, ran forward and hit the spotlight, exploding in six directions – Grace, Drew, Elena going right – Aisha, Israel, Debra going left, as Francy slide into center stage. They thrusted deeply forward, their bodies interpreting the guttural sound of the bass. The crowd screamed in release.

The seven dancers intertwined and hip hopped between each other as one unit flying across the stage. The girls drag their hands up their already sweaty, gyrating bodies and the boys simulated the rhythm of the base alongside them. Now it was the crowd that was sweating, following the dancers every seductive move.

The rhythm dictated their cool, but provocative motion; hips assertive, hands pushing on the offbeat, while heads pop on the 8-count. It was both intricate, mind-blowing choreography along with their self-assuredness which made this sexy seven the "toast of the coast." It was what had earned them the reputation as Miami's own.

The six-minute dance felt like a blink of an eye. As they hit their finale pose, the crowd erupted in applause. "Not bad for three days of rehearsals," Israel commented through his smile.

"We nailed it," Aisha assured.

The dancers run off stage and collapse. "I jumped that last 8-count," Drew confessed.

"I missed the last set of hands," Grace said, "but Elena crushed it."

"You guys were amazing!" Francy confirmed. "Listen to that crowd."

They were still applauding.

The slow clapping of a single individual in the shadows could be heard behind them, further backstage. It caught Israel's ear. "Hey Daphne, you made it." Israel stood up from his position sprawled out on the floor.

"Very impressive." Daphne continued to clap. "You guys killed it."

"Interesting choice of words," Grace commented under her breath.

"How did she know we were performing here tonight?" Elena whispered?

"I might have texted her the info," Israel confessed.

"Social whoring?" Elena smiled.

"I need more Instagram followers," Israel laughed.

"Oh, a million followers aren't enough for you?"

"Thanks for coming," Francy offered. "We appreciate the support."

"Well, I have a VIP table set up for us upstairs. Let me buy you a congratulations drink." Daphne gestured for them to follow her.

The four bodyguards at the VIP room parted for Daphne like Mosses in front of the Red Sea. Her reputation preceded her and there was no one who stood in her way.

A waiter ran over with a bottle of Cristal champagne and poured everyone a bubbly refreshment. "I'm so glad we could do this," Daphne confided. "You were all so wonderful tonight. I can see why this town makes such a big deal about your dance group. Your style and moves are like no other troupe I've ever seen. And I've seen a lot," she chuckled. "Cheers to the Sexy Seven!"

"Chin chin," Israel interrupted. "I really like that name."

"Salut," Aisha added.

The group raised their glasses clinking the flutes of libation in a toast.

"Thanks, Israel, for texting me the information for tonight's event," Daphne smiled. "I've always wanted to catch your act. Katie always tells me about the crowds you draw."

Grace and Aisha shot Israel a "look." "La jaguar," Israel confirmed.

"Well, let's see...I had the pleasure of meeting Drew and Israel last night. I know Ansel is absolutely smitten with Debra... and Francy," Daphne paused... "you used to go out with my mother's boyfriend, Castro, yes?" she asked in a knowing tone.

Caught off guard, Francy, smiled, "Oh that was a long time ago," she confirmed. "Ancient history."

"Elena, I know from the lounge circuit in New York. Thanks for singing at the party. The crowd loved you," Daphne gestured with both arms opened wide.

"But I don't know Aisha and Grace," Daphne said, slowly turning her head towards the last two on the sofa.

"Well, you know our names," Aisha responded, almost taking offense that she was not recognized from her movies.

To change the sudden shift of attitude in the air, Grace blurted out, "We are so sorry about your father's death."

Drew and Debra's heads snapped in Grace's direction. There was automatic silence within the circle. The atmosphere went from casual conversation to what felt like the air had been sucked out of the room.

Daphne's attitude changed. She took a large gulp of champagne and slowly placed the empty glass on the table in front of her. She waved the waiter over to pour her another glass. She waited until he walked away and raised her now full glass. "Good riddance," she smirked.

"He was an awful man," she continued. "He never had any faith in me simply because I am a woman. He didn't think I could run his shipping company and he hated the fact that I'm a lesbian," she concluded.

Dead silence in the circle. The rest of the VIP room was a buzz in chatter and laughter.

"Perhaps he didn't get a chance to know you," Aisha started.

Daphne interrupted her. "No, he's always been a machismo, ignorant swine."

Elena leaned into Drew and whispered, "Ya, but how does she really feel?" Drew gave her a nudge.

"My father thought it more prudent to have Ansel run the company since he was a marine. He found my brother Walter weak and inadequate, and he knew my mother was having an affair with that trainer," she popped her head in Francy's direction. "So, the only one he trusted was Ansel. He just used me and my brother for errands or to make sure we kept the family out of the tabloids."

"I guess that didn't work out," Elena whispered to Drew. He nudged her once again, this time catching Daphne's' attention.

"Oh, I know how people perceive me, but the final straw was him not accepting my sexual orientation. That's when I decided to hook up with Katie. The one girl who had power over him. The girl who is in control of all his movements in and out of the ports of Miami. The CEO of Miami Moves."

"Well, I bet that pissed him off," Grace added with a half-smile, not quite sure what to say.

"It's as if my father and I were always playing chess, seeing which one of us could make the smarter move," Daphne chided. "I guess I had the final say."

This time, Drew nudged Elena. "What does that mean?" Drew thought. "She had the final say in what way?" He knew Elena caught that comment as well.

Just as she made the off-the-cuff remark, Katie Roma entered the VIP lounge. Breezing in with confidence as if she had no care in the world. She greeted the group as she draped her shawl over the sofa. She pulled out of her purse a round disk that she untwisted and in one move, clipped the disk onto the table, and hung her purse off of that. She picked up a champagne flute and gulped the entire glass down. Then she removed her Gucci heels and tossed them in another corner.

"Well, make yourself at home, darling," Daphne suggested. "Why are you so elated?"

"Awww, long day at work," Katie confessed. "I'm so glad it's over."

"You certainly know how to make an entrance," Grace added. "You should join our group."

Debra shot Grace a pair of "evil eyes" across the sofa.

"Francy, how did they dance for you tonight?" Katie cooed.

Francy put on her best show biz smile. "We gave them a great show."

"Drew, you bad boy. You didn't tell me you were performing tonight." Katie almost sounded left out. Before Drew could respond Katie interrupted him. "Darling, do you have an antacid or something? That bubbly is bothering me."

Drew grabbed his bag and handed it to Debra, who handed it to Francy who then gave it to Katie. "Upper pocket," Drew dryly responded.

"We were just talking about you, my dearest," Daphne relayed to Katie.

"Were your ears burning?" Elena joked. "Daphne was just sharing her opinion about her father."

Katie stood up and dropped Drew's bag back in the corner. "Why am I always in the middle of a father-daughter spat?" Katie questioned.

Daphne's face went from thrilled to peeved. "Well, I guess you won't have to worry about that anymore." Daphne picked up her purse and stormed out of the VIP lounge.

"Spoiled rich girl." Drew heard Katie say in a low tone. "Anyone want to dance?" Katie picked up her high heels and slipped them back on as if she couldn't wait to get out of there.

Francy, Alisha, and Grace accompanied Katie downstairs to the massive dance floor.

"Why is it always like fireworks around these people?" Debra suggested as she took off her heels.

"It's the attitude of the rich and privileged," Drew added rolling his eyes. "Speaking of...isn't Ansel picking you up tonight?"

Debra smiled. "Yes, but not until about 2 am. He is going to text me."

CHAPTER 4
WASHINGTON AVE.

THE FOLLOWING MORNING, Aisha was woken up by the incessant ringing of her cellphone.

"Can you believe Ansel didn't have the nerve to even call me or get back to me last night?" Debra was fuming over the phone.

"And good morning to you, mi amor," Aisha managed. "Well, maybe Ansel fell asleep. Did you call him?"

"Yes… many times. Men." Debra huffed.

"He was probably sleeping and didn't hear his phone ring," Aisha was now siding with Ansel. She quickly changed the subject. "That was quit a spat between Daphne and Katie Roma."

"Ohhh that Katie Roma. I don't trust anyone who wears Gucci shoes and a thrift store dress together."

"They are an odd pairing," Aisha confirmed.

"Right?" Debra concurred. "I would never wear that."

"No, Katie and Daphne," Aisha corrected. "Daphne seems so in love, yet Katie doesn't seem to take it too seriously, does she?"

28

"They are always having lover's spats," Debra suggested, her mind distracted. "Katie doesn't seem to know what she wants. Listen, I'll see you in dance rehearsal. Ciao Ciao." She abruptly hung up.

Meanwhile, Drew was headed over to the police station. His curiosity had gotten the best of him, and he thought it was time to check in with an old friend.

Detective Vincent Alasa was a beat cop on patrol in the Broadway district in New York where he and Drew had become acquaintance back in the day. They both worked in proximity to each other. Drew would get Vincent and his then girlfriend tickets to his show, meanwhile Vincent was always there when certain brash fans would become overzealous for autographs at the stage door after each show or when a rash of muggings where prevalent in the Broadway district around 46th street.

A tall lanky Jamaican man in his mid-50s, Vincent had the distinct ability to be the "every man" - down to earth, friendly, and open. But then he could turn off the charm and be a hard-nosed, bull-headed, and persistent man of the law.

Now, a detective with the Miami police department, Vincent was transferred south to warmer shores where he and Drew ran into one another a few years later.

"Hey man, how's it going?" Vincent smiled as Drew entered his office.

"Redecorating?" Drew joked as he looked around noticing the unkept piles of paper, the desk stacked high with books, and the window shades in total disarray.

"Ima regular Ralphy Lauren," he laughed. "Did you just come by to disrespect me, man?" Vincent furled his brow.

The two had the utmost respect for each other. "No sir," Drew confirmed. He led with the car attack on him and Debra.

"Well now, that sounds more like a joy ride gone wrong," Vincent concurred. "But with the little physical description you've given me and no license plate it would be hard for me to find out anything. To my knowledge, we haven't had another attack on file fitting that description."

Drew changed the subject. "You must be working on the investigation of Falcon White's death, yes?"

"Oh, ya. It's all hands-on deck. He was of huge prominence in this town and his business was global."

Although Drew didn't want to push the inquiries, something was bothering him after the very strange night he had on the yacht. "Any suspects?"

Vincent dropped his head and looked down the bridge of his nose. "Now ya know I can't divulge anything of the sort. It's an ongoing investigation."

"Well, I was at his funeral celebration on the families' private yacht the other night and believe me, there wasn't a mourner on deck. It was a full-blown party!" Drew exclaimed.

"Oh really?" Vincent's ears perked up. "By the way... how was it that you came to be at the funeral? How do you know the family?"

"I don't know the family," Drew said matter-of-fact. "I know the girlfriend of Daphne White. Katie Roma. She invited me." Drew suddenly realized that all his friends had been on that ship, but had no idea how that came to be.

"What I can tell you is that there was no love lost in that family," Drew confessed. "Except for Ansel White. He seemed to really love and honor his father."

"Well, the family is always the prime suspect in a brutal murder," Vincent slipped.

"So, it was brutal?" Drew caught him in mid-sentence.

Vincent realized he let the cat out of the bag. "Ok, yes it was a murder."

"Oh, I know," Drew let on. "I got an earful at that funeral. The drunkard twin son, the jealous, hateful younger daughter, the persistent assistant, and the wife who's been having an affair behind her husband's back... And that was just the obvious observations I made."

"I should put you on the case," Vincent joked. "You've observed more in one night than my team has gathered in a week's worth of interviews."

Vincent was very aware of Drew's past at this point. Knowing that as a teenager, his favorite aunt was murdered and the case was never solved, made Vincent very sympathetic to the deep scare that Drew carried with him. With a polite push out the door, Vincent let Drew know, "if something comes up on that car, I'll give you a call."

"Appreciated," Drew echoed back. "I'm late for rehearsal anyway."

Drew left the police station and headed over to the gym. It was particularly quiet for the morning. The gym receptionist greeted him with a smile and he bolted up the steps, thinking in the back of his head that he might be late for rehearsal.

Drew stood there in the doorway of the dance studio, unable to fathom the unspeakable act he was witnessing. The air in the dance studio seemed heavy, almost musky and damp. The rays of sun bathed the room in the most perfect light. The rich spectrum brought out the hues of the space, taking his eyes through a kaleidoscope of vivid color. The light bounced off the natural wood flooring then danced in the air. Its gentle, yet powerful premise reached the thin, sinewy cadaver of a body hanging grotesquely in the air.

Drew's heart quickened in pace as he tried to make sense of what his eyes were taking in. He scanned the room again and again, but his gaze kept coming back to the body he was forced to look at.

The shock and adrenaline were playing with his mind. Drew's body shook internally with a quiver that made his temples pulse. He tried to refocus his view of the detailed account before him.

He looked closer at the body. He noticed the pale white hue of the skin and the fact that Rigor mortis had set in. The veins bulged around the neck, hands, and ankles. He detected arteries that had been cut opened and were now void of blood. The body that was dangling before him was wrapped in the straps suspended from the ceiling, which were usually reserved for the aerial yoga hammocks. The lifeless, contorted body hung upside down.

A shrieking scream pierced his ear from behind. He turned quickly to see the Argentinean heiress, in shock. Debra had her hands squelching the blood-curtailing cry, as her expressive eyes said everything.

"Is that…. Ansel?" she choked.

Drew confirmed her observation. His attention went right back to the corpse he now couldn't take his eyes off of. It was then he noticed tiny droplets of blood caked into the hardwood floor below the body. There were half a dozen droplets of blood that had spread out from the corpse. The blood had a faint smell of copper. Coagulated and dark, these droplets were telling a little more about the tale of this untimely death.

Drew and Debra suddenly heard Francy and Israel laughing in the hallway outside, completely unaware as to what they were about to encounter. Debra quickly dashed out the door to give them fore-warning, unfortunately meeting them at the doorway of the studio.

"Oh my God," Israel gasped.

"Holy shit," Francy echoed. "What happened here?"

"Quick, get him down!" Debra cried.

"Don't touch anything!" Aisha stepped into the studio. "He's already dead. You're not going to help him now. We don't want to disturb the evidence."

"Mita, the Latin Nancy Drew," Debra shouted, raising one hand. Her adrenaline was on overdrive. She was still not comprehending what was before her.

"No, she's right," Francy confirmed. "Everything around us can be evidence. This is a crime scene now. Everybody out!"

"But what if he killed himself?" Debra retorted.

"Corazon, this is not suicide. It's murder." Drew knew what he saw.

Israel was already on the phone with 911.

Francy turned to see Grace and Elena about to enter the studio for rehearsal. "Girls…. rehearsal is cancelled."

"What's going on?" Grace asked, rather startled by Francy's statement.

But Elena knew. Her gaze was already fixed on the horror through the doorway. In shock, she was unable to relay the message to Grace who was still questioning Francy.

"But the rehearsal schedule we have was for today," Grace insisted.

"My dear, Ansel has been murdered," Aisha informed Grace, matter of fact.

"The police are on their way," Israel confirmed.

"Oh my God, Oh my God! Who would do this?" Debra cried. "His eyes…"

Ansel was dressed in a casual chartreuse suit and white shirt that was bathed in dried blood. His eyes remained open. A strong odor had permeated the room. Although paralyzed from shock, Debra and the girls were escorted out of the studio by Israel and Drew just as Detective Vincent entered the gym. He was accompanied by four policeman and a forensic team.

The policeman separated the dancers. Detective Vincent led Drew to the dance studio doorway. "Your friend, who called this in, said you were the one who found the body." Detective Vincent assumed a hardline of questioning. "How did you get in the gym so early?"

"It was open. The receptionist was here and one of the managers," Drew recalled. "I came upstairs and went directly to the studio for rehearsal. That's when I discovered him in the rafters."

"Did you notice anything unusual?" Detective Vincent asked.

"You mean besides a dead man dangling in the ceiling?" Drew said sarcastically. "Sorry, it's the adrenaline. I'm just stifled." His brow was sweating. Tension ran up the back of his neck making his head throb. He had a hundred thoughts running through his mind.

"I understand," Detective Vincent shook his head.

"There seems to be a lack of blood in the studio," Drew suggested.

"He was probably killed somewhere else and dropped here," the detective surmised.

"But, why here? Is the killer sending a message?" Drew kept thinking of Ansel's family. "Now, his family would have to deal with another death. Ansel was the successor to his father's business."

"How do you know that?" Detective Vincent looked around at the dance studio to see if anything else seemed out of place. "The father's will has not been read yet."

"Daphne, Ansel's sister told us this."

"When? On the yacht?" the detective inquired.

"No, at the nightclub last night." Drew confirmed.

"Why are you meeting a suspect of another murder at a night club?"

"I didn't know she was a murder suspect. Besides, she met with us," Drew insisted. "We had a gig at a nightclub last night and Daphne came to see our show."

"Why would she do that?" Detective Vincent was now digging deeper.

"Israel invited her the night of her father's funeral on the yacht, and she decided to come to see the show." Drew assumed. "She had a VIP room set up for us after the performance."

A police officer came over to retrieve Detective Vincent. "Ok Drew, sit tight. I've been summoned by forensics."

Drew looked around the gym. He had a sick feeling in the pit of his stomach. Debra was still being interviewed by a police officer. She was now crying hysterically, probably trying to recall the shocking events that had accumulated over the last 48 hours.

Aisha was with another cop, simply posing and smiling as if she was in front of the cameras, not saying a word.

Grace was rambling on about random strings of events she had experienced to a female police officer, while Elena sat on one of the exercise bikes looking out the large windows facing Washington Ave.

"What did the cops say to you?" Drew asked as Elena turned and smiled.

"We thought living on the beach full-time, in this palm tree paradise was going to be boring. We are surrounded by a hell-of-a-lot more mayhem than we ever saw in New York!"

They were interrupted by the sound of a cell phone ringing. Drew and Elena looked about. The phone kept ringing. The additional policeman in the gym were now looking around to see whose phone continued to intrude on their investigation.

"Are you going to get that Debra?" Detective Vincent walked out of the dance studio on his cell phone.

Debra, completely confused, looked down and realized it was her cell phone sounding the alarm. She stumbled into her bag, searching for the loud intruder. "Hello?" she said with anticipation in her voice.

"It's Detective Vincent. You can hang up now."

More confused than ever, she looked up at the detective who was standing over her. He held up a piece of paper that was in a clear, plastic evidence envelop. "We found this paper in Ansel White's pocket. I rang the phone number to see who would answer and to my surprise, the number rang here in the gym. Care to explain?"

Debra, now feeling like she was being accused, silenced her phone and placed it gently back into her purse. She slowly stood up and looked Vincent straight in the eyes. "He is my fiancé."

"Can you tell me what these numbers and letters are?" Detective Vincent inquired. He flipped the crumbled paper around. Debra looked closer, trying to interpret what she was seeing through the plastic.

She shook her head. "No, I can't."

"Are you the same Debra that was chased by the black sports car?"

Debra looked up into Detective Vincent's eyes. "How do you know about that?" A realization crossed her mind. She looked around the gym to find Drew.

"Yes, Debra. I told Detective Vincent about the incident."

"Do you feel they are related?" Debra questioned.

"Hmmm, it's too early to say," he inferred, rubbing his chin. "Well, Debra, I'm sorry for your loss," Detective Vincent offered his condolences. "I had no idea you were engaged to Ansel White. We'll get to the bottom of this. I'm going to give you a police escort."

"Oh no you're not," Debra insisted. "I'm not going to baby sit some cops. I've got a life and that doesn't include tag-a--longs. Besides, I have six other family members who are always around me. They won't let anything happen to me." As she looked, there were Francy and Aisha, Grace and Israel, Drew and Elena circled around her and the detective.

"I see. You have your family around you. I understand. But I want you all to understand this. Your lives could be in danger. You're somehow involved with some forces that have not yet been revealed, so I want you all to be very cautious," the detective surmised. The forensic team will continue to work here to see if we can determine any further details, but you will need to be hyper aware of your surroundings.

Drew walked with Detective Vincent away from the crowd. "It would have taken more than one person to get Ansel's body up in those rafters," Drew determined.

"We are asking management about keys and who had access," Detective Vincent confirmed. "Yes, it's possible there is another accomplice."

"But why here? Why in the dance studio?" Debra overheard them talking.

"The killer is trying to send a message," Drew concluded.

The group exchanged glances. The detective was called back into the dance studio by the forensic team.

"It feels like we've been violated." Grace sat down on the floor holding her stomach. Her words brought chills to everyone in the group.

"My head is pounding," Debra started to cry. A collective sensation of dread seemed to engulf the room. The seven huddled closer together, their heads hung low.

"Ok, guys, what are we thinking?" Francy jumped in. "Drew, come on, you're the puzzler. What do you see?"

"Why kill the father and the son? What would the killer stand to gain?

"Money? The business? Inheritance?" Israel suggested.

Drew stopped and thought. He looked at his friends who were gathered around. "The Whites may have been in possession of valuable assets, confidential information, or were involved in illegal activities. Killing them could be a way for someone to gain control over their assets or eliminate potential witnesses."

"Could it be a rival shipping company?" Elena interrupted.

Drew closed his eyes. This helped his mind focus. "Maybe there was a dispute or rivalry between the victims and a competitor. Yes, it's possible."

"Perhaps competition for a contract, a client, or other resources," Elena suggested.

"Could the incident with you and Debra and the crazy driver be connected to this?" Grace questioned.

"But why would they want Debra out of the picture?" Aisha stopped and thought. She pondered for a minute and then answered her own question. "Maybe the killer knew Ansel was going to propose to Debra beforehand. So, they wanted Debra out of the way before she complicated matters even more. Is that why we are seemingly being pulled into this?"

"Too late," Grace added with an air of sarcasm. "We are in the middle of this." She clutched her stomach again.

"I think we're missing something," Drew said slowly. "Something important."

"What do you mean?" Francy asked, leaning forward.

"Well, we've been assuming that the killer was motivated by money or rivalry or something like that," Drew explained. "But what if there's a more personal reason behind the murders?"

"What do you mean?" Israel asked.

"Ansel or his father might have been involved in a personal conflict or had enemies who sought revenge," Drew said, shaking his head.

Aisha stood up and pulled her hair back. "This could be due to a personal grudge or an unresolved dispute."

"Such as an act of retaliation or an attempt to settle an old score," Debra chimed in. "It seemed the entire family was against the father," Debra confirmed. "Even Ansel seemed to be on the fence about his father's behavior at times. I mean I could be mad at my family, but I'm not going to kill them!"

Silence fell over the group as they considered the theories. They were dreaded thoughts, but did they make sense?

"Well, forensics puts the time of death at about 1am," Detective Vincent projected, walking out of the dance studio. "Can you tell me where each of you were at that time?"

"We were all together," Drew blurted out. "We were at the club finishing a performance."

"At 1 am?"

"Well, we were done by then, and Daphne White invited us for drinks in the VIP lounge," Grace jumped in, twisting her body, not sure she said the right thing.

"Yes, I heard you were with Daphne White. Does she usually go to your shows?"

"It was her first time seeing us perform," Israel commented.

"Ya, ok bring them over." Detective Vincent motioned to an officer at the top of the steps accompanying the gym manager, the receptionist, and the morning trainer on duty.

"Castro Pryorr," Francy exclaimed.

"Mamacita," Castro slurred as he walked by Francy.

"Hey bar boy!" Castro recognized Israel from the funeral on the yacht.

"So, you three opened the gym this morning at 6am?" Detective Vincent inquired. They nodded their heads yes. "And you're the only one with keys to the gym?" he pointed to the manager. The manager confirmed it so. "And you saw nothing since you've been here?" Detective Vincent asked Castro.

"I don't go in no dance studio," Castro smirked with pride.

"Maybe you should start," Francy quipped.

"Castro nodded his head. "Are we done here officer?"

"Detective. And yes, you are done here."

Castro turned on his heels and blew Francy a kiss.

"You should let Mrs. White know her son is dead," Francy answered him back.

Castro's retort with a half smirk on his face.

Debra looked down at her purse. She heard the faint clamor of her ringer again. She slowly pulled the cellphone out of her bag. Not recognizing the number, she hesitated. "Hello?"

"Hello. Is this Debra?" the gravelly voice asked. Debra could make out the subtle sniffling over the receiver. "This is Mrs. Joyce White," the voice trembled.

Debra's face froze.

"My son Ansel is dead. I need to talk to you."

CHAPTER 5
COCONUT GROVE

DEBRA'S BMW FOLLOWED the tree-lined circular drive that led to the White's palatial estate. As she stepped out of her car, she couldn't help but feel nervous. Mrs. White was known for her sharp tongue and shrewd business sense. The fact that she was willing to meet with Debra meant that she needed something from her. At the request of her friends not to go alone, both Detective Vincent and Debra thought it would be a good opportunity to further both investigations. Debra stepped out of her car, straightened her dress and walked up to the grand entrance of the White mansion.

The doors opened automatically and Debra was greeted by a butler who walked her through the grand hallway, past the countless paintings and sculptures that lined the walls. Debra couldn't help but feel like she was in a museum rather than a private residence.

Finally, the butler led her into a large drawing-room and asked her to wait. Debra sat down on one of the velvet chairs and looked around. The room was stunningly decorated, with antique furniture and an exquisite chandelier hanging from the ceiling. She wondered how much it all cost.

The door opened, and Mrs. White entered the room. She remembered her from the yacht. Happy, dancing, celebrating the death of her husband. Kissing that trainer… She looked completely solemn now.

"Debra, thank you for coming." Joyce White greeted her with a blank look in her eyes. Debra could see her pain and desperation which almost appeared to fill the room behind her.

"Of course, Mrs. White. I'm sorry for your loss." Debra took a seat opposite her and crossed her legs.

"And I'm sorry for your loss. I know Ansel was very fond of you and insisted on marrying you. He said to me that he 'just knew you were the one.' It became even more apparent after his father, Falcon died," Joyce sniveled.

Debra was speechless.

"I know you were close to my son. I was hoping you could shed some light on his murder?" Mrs. White's voice was tight with emotion.

Debra hesitated before speaking, knowing that she was the one who found him dead.

"He was a brilliant man, your son," Debra smiled. "He was always looking out for me. He was supposed to pick me up at work last night, but never showed up. That's when I sensed something was wrong."

"Where was that?" Joyce inquired.

"We had a dance gig downtown last night," Debra shifted in her chair.

"Oh yes, my sweetheart went to see your group, 'The Sexy Seven' perform. I hear about your group often. That's why I wanted your friends on the yacht the other night," Joyce expressed her pleasure of that evening.

"Your sweetheart? Oh yes, Daphne treated all of us to champagne and stimulating conversation." Debra smiled, clinching her jaw.

"She's rather misguided, but she means well," Joyce confided. "It's tough being the only girl around all men. She had to figure a lot out."

Debra quickly changed subjects. "That was quite a fiesta on your yacht the other night. I've never been to a funeral like that before." Debra declined a drink from the butler in mid-conversation.

"Well, listen," Joyce started. "I loved my husband once, but the bigger he became in business, the further apart we became. I finally gave up. He wasn't the same man once he got greedy. Sure, we live well because of it, but at what cost?" The sadness in her heart was palpable. "He turned into an angry, vindictive man."

Debra sat poised as a porcelain doll listening to a second confession from the same family in two days. "That had to be very difficult," Debra added.

Joyce chugged down her second Scotch she garnered from the butler and slammed the glass on the neighboring colonial desk. "He was a monster. Probably because he was being blackmailed." She slipped that bomb into the conversation just as smooth as she knocked back the Scotch.

Debra shifted in her chair again.

"Probably the same person blackmailing him was the one who killed him," Joyce suggested. "That's why I wanted to know if Ansel had knowledge of this and if he did, was he able to confide in you?" Joyce looked down her nose at Debra searching for an answer.

"I'm so sorry, but Ansel never spoke a word of this," Debra confessed. In her mind, Debra knew things did not add up. Why would you kill someone you're blackmailing? It would be like killing your cash cow. Secondly, why would anyone kill Ansel if they are blackmailing the father? Now she wished Drew was with her.

"If your husband was being blackmailed, why didn't he go to the police?" Debra inquired.

"Are you kidding?" Joyce reacted. "Could you imagine the scandal if that was leaked to the public?"

"Do you know what the blackmail was about?" Debra pushed.

Instantaneously, the doors to the drawing-room swung open. "She doesn't want to be disturbed!" Castro Pryorr entered the room attempting to block Lizette, the assistant to Falcon White from entering the room. Debra could see the butler, behind the two of them with his hands up in the air and a look of disgust on his face.

"Maam, I attempted to tell both your staff, that you were occupied," the butler blurted out apologetically.

"Staff?" Castro called out. "You better learn your place!" he barked at the butler. "I'm not the staff. You better get that into your thick skull."

"Castro," Joyce spoke calmly to him. "Please, not today. Lizette, what do you need?"

"I'm sorry Mrs. White. I have some papers for you to sign."

Debra noticed Lizette perspiring from the interaction. Castro stood there, like a bully whose tires were just deflated and the butler seemed to be completely over the entire charade. Debra overheard Joyce asking the butler if Daphne was back from the police station. He shook his head. "No," she could see him whisper.

Castro locked eyes with Debra and slowly walked over to her, circling like a vulture, observing his prey. She sensed his piercing dark eyes scanning her body. "How is it that your fiancé is dead?" he whispered.

She didn't give him the pleasure of an answer. "Just another gold digger after his empire," he snuffed.

She had the best retort but bit her tongue. She didn't want Mrs. White to be concerned with one more argument.

Once Argentina's premier "petite ballerina" Debra left the fold of her family's wealthy wine empire to branch out and be her own, self-made woman. So, she wasn't going to let some sway-back heart throb push her around. She gracefully rose, as any ballerina would, and walked away from him.

Joyce quickly signed the papers Lizette brought her. Lizette then apologized for the intrusion. Lizette looked Debra in the eyes as if to give her a message telepathically, then scurried out of the room with the butler behind her.

Debra was now left alone in the room with the vulture and the cat. Joyce White's jet-black hair complimented her leopard leotard and tights. Debra felt as if she was surrounded.

"So, Debra...." she purred, "what did Ansel tell you?" Her mood had changed. She now seemed less the-perfect-host and more like she was ready to pounce.

"In regard to?"

"The blackmail!" Castro cut her off.

Debra kept her stage fright at bay. Hiding behind her grace, she said calmly, "I just learned about blackmail from you, Mrs. White."

"Why were you meeting with my daughter Daphne at the nightclub?"

"Were you and Ansel blackmailing Falcon White? Did things get out of hand? Did you and your friends kill Ansel?" Castro raised his voice.

Joyce shot Castro a look as she shushed him.

Debra's head was spinning from the accusations coming at her left and right. She stood up. She took a deep breath. "Mrs. White, I realize you lost both your husband and son in the same week. I am sorry for your loss. I think our conversation has concluded."

She turned on her heels to exit the drawing-room. Castro lunged at her in order to stop her from leaving. Joyce grabbed his hand.

Debra didn't look back. She exited stage left and kept going through the double doors, past the countless paintings and sculptures that lined the walls, and through the grand hallway where the butler was holding the door open for her.

She caught a glimpse of Lizette at the top of the stairs as she bolted out the front doors and jumped into her BMW back to the beach.

Debra didn't stop. She drove all the way back to South Beach. Running on adrenaline, all she could do was talk to herself to keep her mind from thinking about what she just went through. She turned on the radio:

> *"Shipping magnate Ansel White, who had inherited his father's notorious legacy, was found murdered in chilling circumstances today. The details of his demise are murky, much like those of his father, Captain Falcon White, who is rumored to have suffered a similar fate a week prior. The White family's prodigal son, once praised for his valorous service as a marine, was discovered by his fiancé, Debra Arditi, in a scene that left more questions than answers."*

Meanwhile, Aisha had ideas of her own. She wanted to know who was targeting her friend. She followed Debra to the White's mansion in Coconut Grove. When Debra went on to the grounds, Aisha headed for the service entrance. She was out to get answers and wanted to make sure Debra was being watched over.

Aisha loved good drama and tantalizing mysteries. Famous for her films in Spain, this beguiling actress used her power to get what she needed and let the press do the rest.

Coyly hiding behind that bright white show biz smile, Aisha was a powerhouse of energy. When she was excited, she talked a mile a minute. When she was confident, she just smiled, hiding all that mischief and self-empowerment in one tight little package.

She gained military tactics training from her Mossad coach for her last film, so she knew how to handle weapons. Any weapon. But she chose to use her lipstick as her most powerful ally.

She parked outside the service entrance gate of the mansion and walked up to the security guard. *"Hola guapo,"* she addresses the handsome Latin guard. *"Disculpame, pero,* I'm having a little car trouble," she pouted.

The guard looked her up and down. He hesitated. Once he assumed she didn't seem like a threat, he responded, *"Que paso?"*

She switched to English. She knew she had to get him out of his little guard booth. "The car just keeps stopping and starting," she said tossing her arms up in the air.

The guard looked around to make sure there was nothing suspicious around him. He stepped out of the booth and moved cautiously towards her. Aisha caught glimpse of a pistol strapped to his waist.

"Nice Glock," she commented. He looked down at his holstered gun.

"You know about these?" he asked, surprised.

She just smiled.

As he walked around the car, Aisha observed her surroundings. Shipping containers lined the back garden wall. Workers were shuttling crates of vegetables and fresh flowers into the house. The massive white home had red and purple bougainvillea growing up the backside covering almost three-quarters of the pristine wall. Two gardeners scampered about filling in a large hole with dirt, after planting a 10-foot palm tree they had just secured into the earth.

"Who lives here?" she enquired to the guard, who was now face up under the center of her car. She noticed his big legs and combat boots squirming under the carriage, fussing with some wires, which she deliberately disconnected herself earlier.

"Not sure if this will do it, but you had some wires loose under there, which probably has to do with the computer system in your car," he smiled as he crawled out from underneath. "It's the White's mansion. You know, the shipping tycoon."

"No," Aisha lied, " I have no idea." She hesitated, hoping she could buy more time in order to discover something that made sense in her surroundings. She desperately looked around as she got back into the driver's seat. She started her car. "Wow, it even sounds better. *Tu sabes mucho!*" She thanked him in Spanish.

"You can turn around here." The guard motioned for Aisha to pull further in through the gateway. Her car advanced forward up over the lip of the elevated driveway. In front of her were three vehicles being washed by a worker in overalls. A red Ford truck, a white GM van, and a black Mazda sports car with tinted windows. The hood's ornament was missing, but Aisha knew her vehicles. She stopped her car and quickly jumped out and walked around to the back of the black Mazda to make note of the Florida license plate. "Gotcha," she said to herself.

She got back into her car and quickly backed up as she headed out towards the street. *"Oye,"* she got the guard's attention. "I love that Black Mazda," she smiled. "You should tell Mr. White; he's missing his hood ornament."

"Oh, that's not Mr. White's car," the guard informed her.

Before he could finish his conversation, the phone in the guard booth started ringing. The brash bell caused the guard to make an agitated expression as he quickly retrieved the receiver.

Aisha, in fear of being discovered, quickly waved to the guard as she drove down the driveway into the street.

She cleared the large gate and turned slowly onto the road back to South Beach. Suddenly, to her utter surprise, the black sports car pulled out behind her. Aisha quickly pulled over to the side of the road.

As the car rushed by her, she still couldn't see the driver through the tinted windows, but it didn't stop her from going after them. Now, with determination in her eyes, Aisha was in hot pursuit.

CHAPTER 6
BAL HARBOUR

BAL HARBOUR WAS an upscale shopping venue situated on the northern most end of Miami Beach. Known for its extremely high-end retailers and chic restaurants, it made for the perfect spot for people watching. The open-air esplanade was cascading with waterfalls and huge tropical plants, enormous palm trees, and an exquisite crowd. Aisha was already on her cell phone calling Drew.

"Drew, I've just followed that black sports car with the missing hood ornament that tried to run down you and Debra the other day. I've followed them to Bal Harbor."

"Elena, Israel, and I are on our way," Drew responded. "Keep us posted."

Aisha felt as if she was back in Spain filming one of her movies. She loved the intrigue, and on top of this, she felt she was born for this spy game.

The black sports car sped around the corner and idled in front of the valet parking attendant. Aisha watched with anticipation. She observed the driver roll down the window and inquire about something, but her car was at the wrong angle to see inside the mysterious vehicle.

The parking attendant was now in a heated debate with the driver. He was flailing his hands in the air, not seeming to be able to communicate with the persistent driver.

The car door swung open. Lizette Brown stepped out from behind the wheel and shimmied her white mini skirt down her long legs. She raised her car keys in the air and dropped them into the parking attendant's hands. He juggled to keep them from falling on the ground. He handed her a ticket, which she flicked from his hands as she slid her designer sunglasses onto her face and scurried into the shopping venue.

Aisha's was on the phone to Drew. "This just got interesting." She revealed the news.

"We are almost there," Drew exclaimed. "We are just on the other side of the mall. We are driving up to the second level. That's where the valets park the cars. Aisha, can you follow Lizette?"

"Claro," Aisha confirmed. "I just valet parked, and I'm on foot as we speak."

Drew, Elena, and Israel wound their way up the spiral drive leading to the second-floor parking garage.

"Drop me at the elevators," Elena suggested. "I'm going to be a second set of eyes for Aisha."

"Good idea," Drew confirmed. As he pulled over to let Elena out of the car, Drew immediately eyed the black sports car with the valet attendant at the wheel. The valet pulled the car into a vacant spot, rolled up the window, and jumped out of the car.

Drew pulled his car over to the side. Israel jumped out of the back and on to his skateboard. With one push, he was sailing down the asphalt, crouched down as not to be seen by the parking attendants at the nearby booth. Drew followed on foot, like a stealth fighter on a mission.

"The car looks like the same one that came after Debra and I," Drew asserted. "Same missing hood ornament, same tinted windows, and what appeared to be a similar make and model." Aisha had already texted the license plate number to Drew, who, in turn, texted it to Detective Vincent.

"Let's look inside," Israel suggested. Before Drew knew it, Israel had pulled out a long metal instrument from his backpack and inserted it alongside the car window opposite the lock on the driver's side. He worked the tool up and down, gently maneuvering the flat stick back and forth until the door snapped open.

"It looks like you may have done this a few times before," Drew said to Israel, raising one eyebrow.

Israel shrugged his shoulders, chased by that famously innocent smile that could make anyone melt.

"Ya, ya..." Drew laughed.

They knelt in front of the driver's side door and Israel slowly opened it. Drew slid inside and sat crouched behind the wheel.

"What is this girl up to?" Drew questioned, observing every nook and cranny, every button and lever, as he checked under both sun visors. He arched behind him to observe the back seat. His eye caught a bright shiny stone on the floor reflecting the light. He scooped it up and pushed it into his pocket. "Well, this might be something," Drew told himself. He noticed one of the valet attendants looking towards the car.

"Israel, time to boogie," Drew whispered.

Drew noticed a peculiar smell as he slipped out of the front car seat. It had the scent of familiarity, yet he couldn't place it. It was time to bounce before they were both discovered.

———————◆———————

The elevator door opened. Elena breezed out; her eyes tucked behind her black Wayfarers. She had that New York swagger that seemed to fit in anywhere. It was called confidence. She strolled through the esplanade on the lookout for anything suspicious.

"Hey, aren't you the singer from my dad's funeral?"

Elena froze. She quickly did the math in her head. It was a male voice, a dad's funeral, and there were only two siblings left from the only funeral she ever sang at. She turned around and greeted him, like an old friend. "Walter, you sweet thing. It's been a while," she smiled.

"I have to say, you sounded just wonderful at my dad's funeral. Your voice is like velvet," Walter complimented.

"Well thank you," she said coyly.

"Tell me your name again?"

"Elena," she responded quickly. She grabbed his arm as they walked slowly, remembering he had a limp. "Listen, I'm so sorry about your brother. I only met him briefly, but he seemed like a nice man" she said, fishing for a reaction.

Walter's mood changed instantly. "I can't believe what is happening," he mumbled. "Life has just been turned upside down..." he hesitated. "There is a killer running loose and the police don't seem to be doing anything about it. They just harass my family, assuming one of us had something to do with both my father and my brother's death."

"Terrible," Elena reacted. She looked up and, in the distance, she spotted her blond cohort hiding behind big round sunglasses peering into the windows of the Hillstone restaurant.

Elena reacted, "Oh how marvelous." She stopped and turn Walter towards the window at Tiffanys so that he would not see Aisha across the court yard.

"Do you like that bracelet?" Walter asked. Elena did a double take. She had not singled out any piece of jewelry specifically when she pretended to use her reaction as a deflection.

She stopped. "Oh, it's beautiful," she responded not looking at the bracelet, but instead looking for Aisha behind her in the reflection of the shop's window.

Walter tightened his grip around Elena's arm and escorted her into Tiffanys.

Aisha glared through the restaurant's floor to ceiling windows. She followed Lizette to a very trendy restaurant and watched her sit at a large table alone. She observed her behavior while speed dialing Drew.

"That was a close call," Israel commented as he jumped off his skateboard by Drew's car.

"Aisha, what's up?" Drew quickly answered his phone. "Israel, let's go!"

"Walter, that's breathtaking," Elena gasped, "but I can't accept that." The gentleman behind the counter was offering Elena the opportunity to try on the diamond-studded bracelet Walter thought she admired.

"Just try it on," Walter pleaded.

"It would look beautiful on your skin," the salesman insisted.

Elena hesitantly maneuvered the expensive piece of jewelry over her hand and let it adorn her right wrist, diamonds glistening in the showroom lights.

"Walter, it really is a wonderful piece, but I simply cannot accept this," she pressed, her moral dilemma pandering to her sense of decency.

The salesman lightly adjusted the bracelet on her wrist and leaned in to whisper in Elena's ear. "I'm sure you can find it in your heart to accept this immaculate gift from this gentleman who just adores giving."

"I insist," Walter implored. "You did such a beautiful job at my father's funeral. Young man, please wrap that up in your special blue box!"

"Certainly Mr. White," the salesman quickly responded.

Elena reacted to the salesman knowing who Walter was, but said nothing. They strolled out of Tiffanys. Elena, a diamond bracelet sweeter, and Walter, a happier man. "Come join me for lunch?" Walter asked.

Elena wasn't sure what she was getting into, but before she could answer, he added. "I have to meet my father's assistant, but I don't think she would mind."

Elena quickly contemplating her odds. 'Better to be a fly at the table, than a fly on the wall,' she deciphered to herself. "Very good. I'll lunch with you both."

They entered Hillstone's restaurant. It was a bustling array of senses. Soft white curtains separated Maplewood tables accented with smooth Priestley chairs. The scent of grilled steak blended with the colorful salads that flew by on trimly squared dishes serenaded by the pops from champagne bottles constantly firing.

Drew and Israel were candidly shocked to see Elena standing arm and arm with Walter White at the hostess desk. They quickened their pace and made an entrance.

"Elena!" Drew chimed affectionately.

"Drew, what a pleasant surprise," Elena parled. She had no time to explain what happened when she went to assist Aisha. "Of course, you remember Walter?"

"Of course," Drew smiled. Israel, myself, and our other friends met you at your father's funeral," Drew reminded him, as he shook his hand.

"If I remember correctly, you were the one who practically ran me down trying to vomit over the side," Israel laughed, uncomfortably.

Drew quickly gave Israel one of his famous looks, dropping his head and staring him down with wide eyes. "So much for subtlety," Drew nodded.

"That wasn't my best night," Walter confessed. "I was dumb drunk."

That got a knee-jerk reaction out of Elena. "No?!?

Drew turned and shot her the same look. 'Everyone's sarcastic in this bunch,' He thought. 'Did they get that from me?'

"Well, you must join us for lunch. I have to make it up to you," Walter insisted. "Miss, my party has just expanded," he relayed to the hostess.

"Mr. White, your father's assistant has been waiting. We sat her at your usual table," the hostess confirmed.

"That's great. It will be big enough for all of us." Walter gestured to Elena to follow the hostess who was already on her way to lead them to the large table Walter would always reserve.

Lizette Brown stood up. Again, shimming her white mini skirt over her long legs. "Walter, I'm sorry. I apologize. I didn't realize you were having guests. I recognize all of you."

Drew attempted to interpret Lizette's body language as she greeted everyone. Was she the mad motorist with the killer car? Drew got a text. He quickly looked at his phone. It was from Detective Vincent.

"License plate confirmed. Lizette Brown." Drew swallowed hard, trying to contain the news from the detective.

"I'm actually glad you are here," Lizette started. "I saw Debra at the White's mansion this morning. She was getting the third degree from Mrs. White."

"My mom has been out of control for a long time," Walter admitted. "She's running around with a guy half her age. She was practically relieved by the death of my father, and she is now devastated by the death of my brother... making all kinds of accusations."

"Walter, I think we should be a little more discreet," Lizette chided his comments. "But, yes, there is something very scary going on. I tried to warn Debra that she was walking into an inquisition, but I was not able to speak directly to her."

Drew's mind was racing. 'Yet, Lizette was the one who tried to end both Debra and his life not that long ago,' he thought. "Can I ask you where you were on the morning of Captain White's funeral?"

Lizette hesitated. Her eyes darted around the room.

Walter responded. "We were all celebrating Daphne's birthday at the Savoy on Ocean Drive."

"That's an early time of day for a birthday party," Elena suggested.

"No, we were all there from the night before," Lizette recalled. "The party started at 11pm and spilled into the morning hours."

"Wow, so you celebrated a birthday and a funeral within 48 hours!" Israel commented.

"Daphne insisted we continue with the birthday party. She hated her father, so it also represented a very liberating event for her," Lizette said, sadly.

"I was just so distraught. I had scheduled Captain White's "event" that night, forgetting it was Daphne's birthday the night before."

"And was everyone from the family at the party that evening?" Drew inquired.

Lizette and Walter looked at each other. A simultaneous "yes" was their answer.

"And were you there, Lizette? How about Katie and Castro?"

"Yes, we were all there." Lizette recounted the night. "It was another explosive evening. Or should I say morning. Katie was arguing with Daphne. Castro was ducking in and out on Mrs. White, probably flirting with a waitress. Mrs. White was furious with him. Then, Ansel decided to announce that he was going to propose to your friend, Debra. This made Mrs. White more furious.

"And I was experiencing such guilt that night," Walter admitted. "I felt I was the cause of my father's death."

"Were you?" Elena interrupted, coyly smiling. "Sorry, that just came out."

The table became silent. "Walter, what do you mean?" Drew asked, calmly.

The waitress came to the table. "Let's order a little 'Dutch Courage' shall we?" Walter ordered white wine and the spinach dip for the table and sent her off. "I have a confession to make," Walter leaned into the table. "I didn't tell the police that I drove my father to the docks the night he was killed. I was afraid they would accuse me of murdering him."

There were looks exchanged at the table. Drew felt it was his golden opportunity to dig deeper into Falcon White's murder. "Walter, why did you drive your father to the docks in the middle of the night?"

Elena was sitting next to Walter and gave an encouraging squeeze to his arm. "Go ahead Walter, you can talk to us. We are somehow involved in this. We were the ones who found your brother Ansel's body."

Walter looked at Elena. His face registered genuine shock. "The detective told me it was his fiancé who found him?"

"We were all with Debra when we discovered him in our dance studio," Drew confided.

"My father told me he had a very important business dealing that couldn't wait for the morning. He insisted I drive him that night."

"Did he tell you who he was meeting?" Drew pushed.

"No. He never explained much to me."

"Lizette, you were Captain White's assistant. Did he tell you who he was meeting?" Drew didn't expect a straight answer from her, suspecting she was somehow involved.

"I knew he had a meeting that was called very suddenly on the night he was killed. He wrote down information that I was supposed to give to Ansel.

"Ansel?" Walter repeated. "Well, my father gave me something too!" Walter told the group. "He trusted me too, you know," he smirked in a jealous tone.

Israel reached for the spinach dip and tortilla chips, which broke the immediate tension at the table. Walter poured wine in everyone's glasses. Elena leaned over to Drew, "Lizette could be misleading us," she whispered.

"What information did you have for Ansel?" Elena casually asked Lizette as she took a big gulp of wine.

"That's private," Lizette stated. "But I know there was something shady going on within the family business. Captain White had a lot of secrecy around him. The bigger his business got, the more secrets I had to try to decipher, as he would never tell me directly what was happening. He became increasingly paranoid with his competitors. He was constantly talking to himself about Miami Moves and spent countless hours in his office. He even slept there occasionally."

"Well, who would go home if your wife was sleeping with her trainer," Israel blurted out as he thoroughly enjoyed the spinach dip.

Elena kick Israel under the table. "Why Miami Moves?"

"They are the head of operations at the port of Miami and Katie Roma is the one who controls all of that. So, Captain White was always at odds with her. He would demand more port rights or better timing on the docks for his ships and Katie didn't stand in his way for a long time. She was almost passive to his demands, until Daphne came into the picture and started dating Katie. It was as if they were playing chess."

"I bet that infuriated Captain White," Drew added.

"Between Ansel, Captain White, and Katie, there was always a triangle of tension," Lizette confirmed.

Drew turned to Elena. "I think it's time we visit Katie Roma at Miami Moves.

CHAPTER 7
PORT OF MIAMI

THE SUN BREECHED the lip of the horizon just in time to assert its best morning glow across the azure water, made even more beautiful by the Gulf Stream. It was one of the most endearing trademarks of South Beach. Pristine beach air meandered across their faces as Francy, Grace, and Drew made their way to their breakfast meeting with Katie Roma.

"I'm so glad she agreed to meet us," Grace said as she pulled back her long green braids and tied them up in a Versace scarf.

"We try to meet over a meal a couple times a month," Drew confirmed. "So, this isn't really out of the ordinary."

"But will she be open to the fact that you have two tag-a-longs?" Francy asked.

"I told her Grace and I had an early morning exercise class with you, Francy, so she was accommodating."

Miami Moves was a gigantic warehouse like space. After a security check in the lobby of the building, the trio made their way upward in the massive, glass elevators. They entered a huge control room on the top floor. It reminded Drew of NASA's control center. Over 100 operators were fixated on a large screen in the front of the room. The active port was not only managing international trade ships coming in and out of the waters off the coast of Miami, but over 25 cruise ships had to be maneuvered through the seaport, seamlessly without conflict or traffic jams.

"Drew, punctual as usual," Katie met them at the door to her office. "No problem with security at the front?"

Drew shook his head.

"I have arranged breakfast on our rooftop café," she smiled. "Hello Francy. I keep telling myself I am going to take your kick-ass class, but I never seem to be able to make it there so early."

Francy admired Katie. She was a powerful, successful woman, which mirrored Francy's mindset and ambitions. "You've really created an empire here," Francy complimented.

"Well, the Port of Miami has a lot of politics and not only that, but there is also a strong, machismo attitude around here. But guess what?" She twisted her chunky designer belt that gathered her vibrant floral dress together like a corset, "I'm stronger!"

"That a girl!" Grace added. "You've created magic here."

They reached the roof and walked astride along the extended wooden deck, which led to a beautiful garden-like setting, covered with large umbrellas and cooling fans blowing air on each table. They sat down to an exquisitely plated composition of fresh tropical fruits, yogurt, and aromatic Cuban coffee satiating the air.

"Drew and I try to do this a few times each month. It doesn't always work out, but its nicer than chit-chatting in that sweat-saturated gym all the time."

"Katie was the first person I met when I moved to Miami full time," Drew initiated.

"Drew is more established in his life now," Katie observed. "He saved money from every dance job to buy a condo in Miami. It seemed to be a life goal but in reality, I think he originally just wanted a place to run to for the winters."

"Miami not only offered warm weather year-round, but the quality of life is so much better than New York," Drew confessed.

"He was so afraid to let go of New York," Katie laughed. "Then I showed him your class, Francy."

"Well, we are all grateful you did," Francy smiled, as she savored a long sip of delicious coffee.

The topic quickly turned to the White murders. "Katie, I know you have been right in the middle of all of this. It must be so difficult dealing with so many emotions."

"It is doubly difficult, as I'm not only involved with Daphne, but I worked indirectly with Falcon White." Katie's tone became rather somber. "Now, with double tragedy in the family, its pure madness."

"Katie, I have to ask," Grace interjected, "that is a beautiful ring. Did you find that here in the States?"

"It's my engagement ring. Daphne proposed last year. It's from Tiffanys." The girls ogled the huge diamond set in a four-pronged setting with a platinum, snake-like band.

"How's Daphne doing?" Drew asked.

"She's crazy as ever," Katie crinkled her forehead. "She wants to have our wedding ceremony soon."

"Wow, no grass grows under her feet," Francy observed. "First a birthday party, then a funeral, and the tragic death of her brother. I'm not sure how she is still standing. But, wanting to plan a wedding?"

"Like I said, madness. How did you know about the birthday?" Katie asked. Her attention refocused.

"We just happened to have lunch with Walter and Falcon White's assistant, Lizette," Drew added. He was curious to see the reaction and his hunch paid off.

"Hmmm. One more inept than the other," Katie shrugged. "Walter squanders the family fortune away on booze, girls, and expensive jewelry, while the other one dedicated her life to a very unstable man."

Drew read into Katie's comments. Her reaction said a lot. It also revealed how she felt about the weaker links in the family chain.

"I'm not a fan of those who are lazy or those who are misguided."

Katie was clearly referring to Walter and Lizette. She changed the subject. "Drew, have you been back to New York lately?"

"No, I'm giving it some space."

They finished their leisurely breakfast and headed downstairs from the rooftop café to Katie's work space. The spacious corner office on the top floor was filled with sunlight streaming through the floor-to-ceiling windows overlooking the ocean. The room was pristine. No clutter, no unnecessary ornaments gathering dust.

"Wow, not even a tchotchke!" Elena remarked. "They are gorgeous flowers."

A huge bouquet of white lilies, pink peonies, white roses, and an accent of red ginger lotus sat on Katie's desk in one corner. She had an open laptop in the center of her work surface and several files piled on the upper right corner.

Drew quickly did a double take. The white lightning streak on a red background caught his eye, peeking out from one of Katie's files. He had seen that before. He quickly ran through the past week's events trying to place, where he saw that image.

"Well, Katie, between you and me, what do you think about this blackmail theory?" Drew asked.

Katie stopped what she was doing. Her shoulders seemed to tense as she looked up from her desk. "What do you mean by blackmail theory?" Katie asked, a concerned look on her face.

"After Ansel's murder, Debra received a phone call from Joyce White. She invited Debra to the mansion essentially to accuse her and Ansel of blackmailing Ansel's father."

"Really?" Katie questioned. "And do the police know about this theory?"

Drew responded, "I think they do. Of course, it's a preposterous theory because Debra had nothing to do with this."

Katie looked back at the papers on her desk, shaking her head in a rather disagreeing way. "Are you sure about that?" There was certainly some type of tension between Katie and Debra, yet Debra never explained. All she would ever say to Drew was that she didn't trust Katie. "I wouldn't have put anything past Ansel," Katie shrugged. "He'd do whatever it took to get what he wanted. Maybe Debra is the same way. Two peas in a pod."

The room was silent except for the deep wailing of a ship's bull horn that could be heard muffled through the thick window pane. Francy and Grace both sent Drew an intense look from the other side of the room.

"It seems like you and Debra just don't get along." Drew slide the comment in to see how Katie would react. There was no response.

"You should look into Manford Grove Industries," Katie hinted. "Ansel and Manford Grove used to work together."

"Castro used to work for Manford Grove too," Francy recalled. "When Castro and I were dating, he was working for Manford Grove on the docks"

"You dated Castro?" Katie reacted in rather disbelief.

"Yes," Francy admitted. "A lapse in judgment. But I finally got him off the docks, and that's how he became a trainer."

"Katie, you seem to know so much, being the Queen of Miami," Drew flattered her. "How was it that Ansel White and Manford Grove were working together? They were rival families in a very competitive industry?"

"Ansel and his father seldom saw eye to eye," Katie divulged. "At one point, Ansel went his own way and joined up with Manford Grove to compete against his father."

"I bet that made waves in the family business," Grace suggested tossing her green braids from one side to the other.

"Falcon never seemed to really trust his son again."

"I thought Ansel was the golden boy of the company?" Drew suggested.

"Well, that is how he was perceived in the media. Ansel was a decorated marine. He was disciplined and a leader. He was respected by the community and the apparent heir to a family fortune," Katie explained as her desk phone rang. "If you'll excuse me," Katie pardoned.

"Katie, thanks for breakfast," Drew bowed, palms pressed together. "We'll see ourselves out."

Francy and Grace gave Katie a quick peck on either cheek as the three dancers dashed out the office door.

"A new twist in the family tree," Grace commented.

"You know," Drew said, thinking out loud, "we are already here. Why don't we snoop around a little bit. Maybe we can find Manford Grove."

Already beyond the security gates, the trio navigated through the long, twisting halls of the labyrinthine complex, leading them into the bowels of Miami's most vital lifeline. From the higher levels, they slowly descended downwards and approached the docks beneath. They passed through floors, which shifted from sleek, contemporary offices filled with high-society executives to blue-collar drones bustling to-and-fro in their plain overalls, uniforms, and work boots. The pungent smell of the sea grew stronger with each step, lending an air of gritty mystery to their clandestine mission.

As they walked through a sturdy ground floor door, the hustle and bustle of the docks unfolded in front of them. A sea of busy workers unloaded huge container ships that had just arrived from destinations far and wide. Two large cranes loomed overhead, their long robotic arms delicately lifting massive metal shipping containers from one location to another. Shouts of instructions echoed throughout the area as forklifts whizzed by carrying crates of merchandise on massive pallets.

"Hey, yews tree need hard hats. What's wrong 'wich you?" An almost unintelligible security guard walked up to the dancers and quickly informed them of the rules.

"I guess we missed that sign," Drew smiled.

"Get 'em ova there," he commanded. The guard pointed to a security booth.

"Thank you, we'll do that," Drew remarked. "By the way, can you point us to Manford Grove's office?"

"Corporate?" He pointed upwards. "Dock traffic?" He pointed further down along the docks. "Now get them hard hats on!" he scolded.

They scuddled further down the wet docks trying to get a foot hold on the wooden planks moistened by sea water. "Look, there is the White family's docking office." They peered through the large dirty window to see Walter White sitting at a desk doing paperwork. Then, an image caught Drew's attention. The logo of the white lightning streak on a red background. It was the logo to the White family shipping company. *White Lightning Shipping.* Drew made the connection. "So, the flash drive, Israel and I found on the boat during the funeral, was property of the White family," he told himself.

"Hey Mr. Drew," Walter rang out. "What are you doing here?"

Drew quickly straightened up from his crouched position at the window. He swiftly motioned to the girls to keep moving down the docks to find Manford Grove's office while he dealt with Walter.

"Hi Walter," Drew greeted him. "Working hard?"

"I've been attempting to make sense of all this paperwork that both Ansel and my father left us with. It's been a nightmare. Hey, how did you get down to the docks here?" Walter asked with a confused look on his face.

"We had lunch with Katie Roma," Drew smiled.

"She is always getting into everyone's business," was Walter's quick reaction. A smug look came across his face. "Just because she owns practically the whole port, it doesn't give her the right."

"It doesn't give her what rights?" Drew said leading Walter on in conversation.

Walter rolled his eyes up in his head and looked away. "Say…how is Miss Elena?"

"Miss Elena? Oh, she's peachy keen," Drew responded with a hint of sarcasm. Drew rapidly changed the subject. "So, you need to go past security to get to the docks at all hours of the night?" Drew inquired.

Walter looked at Drew with a blank stare.

"I'm just curious. You said you drove your father to the docks the night of his murder. If you had to be admitted by the guard, perhaps the killer did too."

"I went over this with the police," Walter huffed. "The killer had to be waiting here for my father when he got here. My father checked in with the front security at midnight."

"Wasn't that an unusual time to be here?" Drew inquired.

"You don't know the shipping business. These ports are going all day and all night. It's not unusual. There are day and night shifts. Yes, it was out of the ordinary for my father to be here that late, but as I said before, he had an important meeting," Walter reiterated. He paused and sat down in his chair. He leaned back and scratched his head. "Say," he hesitated. "What are you, a detective now?"

Drew's posture changed. He cleared his throat in an attempt to come up with a good answer. "Listen, Walter I am concerned. My friend and I were almost run down by a car that happened to belong to someone in your inner circle. My friend Debra's fiancé, your brother Ansel, was murdered and his body left in our dance studio. Debra is being threatened by someone else in your inner circle accusing her of blackmail and murder. So, yes..." he now responded with self-assuredness, "I am playing detective. My friends could be in danger as well as your family. You said at lunch that your father *gave you something too.'* What did you mean by that?"

Walter thought hard for a minute. "Oh, yes," he recalled "It was a flash drive. But stupidly, I lost it."

"What was on the flash drive, Walter?"

"I don't know, but my father gave it to me before he got out of the car for his meeting. He told me to keep it close as it had valuable information on it and he didn't want to take it to his meeting," Walter confessed. Unfortunately, I failed him...again."

Drew kept tight lipped about the flash drive him and Israel discovered. Not knowing who to trust, he quickly changed the subject. "Lizette said your father gave her information she was supposed to give to Ansel. Do you know what that information was?"

"I don't, but I know it had something to do with the flash drive."

"And Lizette...do you trust her Walter?"

Walter paused again, as if he were running the events of the last couple of weeks through his mind trying to decipher the answer to the question. "Lizette was my father's trusted assistant. She was with him for many, many years. She is not a nervous person and could usually handle the craziness that was my father, but once in a while, I could see the stress in her face when my father would bark orders at her. But, dishonest? I don't think so," he decided. "Her and Ansel didn't have the best relationship, though. But I think that's because when Ansel left the family business to work with the competition, Ansel become the enemy. She harbored the same feelings my father did."

Grace and Francy found Manford Grove's docking office. It was only a few paces down from the White's office and bustling with action inside. "We can't just walk in there and ask for Manford Grove," Grace panicked.

"Don't worry," Francy reassured her, "I have an idea."

Francy had the audacity of a five-star general and the ability to think on her feet. They opened the door to the office and the occupants all stopped to look at them.

"Are you lost little girl?" one man commented.

"I think you have the wrong office," another suggested.

"Certainly not!" Francy commanded. "We have an appointment with Manford Grove. We are Katie Roma's assistants," she said convincingly.

Grace got into the act. "And we don't have all day."

"I'm sorry miss," a voice popped out from behind a large floor crate. "We rarely ever get any visitors down here on the docks and especially in this office. I'm Carson Rodriquez. Mr. Grove's assistant. I wasn't aware that he had an appointment," Carson stated.

The girls shook his hand. They stood their ground like soldiers on a battlefield. They were not backing down.

"It was last minute and Katie sent us down here to find him." Francy lied.

"Ok, let me check if he is still in the back office," Carson responded and hurried off through the back door.

"Now what do we do?" Grace asked leaning into Francy. "I don't want to be sent down the river, packing." She was so afraid to be found out that she was now shaking in her shoes.

"Just relax. Breathe." Francy's calm exterior was a façade for her racing mind. She was mentally mapping out all the ways the conversation could go.

A 300-pound man burst through the back door. "What does this confounded woman want from me now?" Manford Grove screamed, wiping the sweat from his saturated forehead. His Southern accent and extreme demeanor overpowered the office. The other workers in the room quickly moved out of his way to give this audacious man some space.

"She simply wanted to let you know about Ansel's funeral," Francy said respectfully.

Grace looked at Francy with a straight face. She quickly turned to Manford Grove, "Are you able to make it?" she added.

Manford Grove shook his head and mumbled some incoherent words. "Where is it going to be? Miami City Cemetery?" he scoffed.

"Where else?" Francy added. "The most famous cemetery in Miami."

"The family would tar and feather me on the spot," Manford said. "I had a lot of respect for that boy. He was practically like a son to me. When is the funeral?"

Francy shifted in her shoes, trying to think of another lie. Grace stalled. "Mr. Grove, may I just ask you, what was it that allowed you to bring Ansel, your competition's son, into business with you?"

A look of sincerity suddenly came over his face. He pondered the question as he slowly sat down in a large, oversized office chair. The wheels squeaked as he leaned back, the chair gracefully accepting his weight.

"That's an odd question," he stated. "When Falcon White became more and more obsessive and compulsive, it pushed Ansel away. They were always disagreeing in business matters. But, when Falcon White tried to burn down his son's office with him in it, that was the last straw for Ansel."

The girl's looked at each other in disbelief.

"Ansel left the family business and came to work with me as a partner. He brought many of the families' clients over to me." Manford seemed to chuckle under his breath, rather enjoying the conquest over his competitor. Then, in the same moment, his face changed again. "But it didn't last long."

"Why not?" Grace interrupted.

"Ansel went back to his family business; minus the clients he brought me. That was enough to bring *Manford Grove Industries* neck and neck with *White Lightning Shipping*. The old man was never the same." Manford sat back again in his squeaky chair cajoling about his victory over Falcon White.

"Well, thank you for sharing that story," Francy admitted.

"Very appreciated," Grace smiled. "Well, we best be on our way."

As the girls turned to leave, the front door swung open in their faces.

"What are you two doing here?" Castro loomed in the doorway, blocking the girls from making a quick exit.

CHAPTER 8
LINCOLN ROAD

THE GIRLS FROZE in their tracks. Francy, quick on her toes reacted. "I think the question is, what are you doing here?"

Castro stood in the doorway, observing the trio in front of him. His sweat pearled on his tanned skin as he pulled off his mirrored sunglasses.

"So, you just decide to show up for your paycheck?" Manford struggled, but managed to get out of his office chair. "Carson?" Manford called out to his assistant. "Get this man his greenbacks!"

"Paycheck? You're still working here?" Francy asked Castro. He pushed passed the girls and snatched his paycheck out of Carson's hand.

"Just barely," Manford added. "He shows up when he wants to and thinks that's OK."

Seeing Castro still triggered something in Francy. She still had feelings for him. But she only had to have her heart broken once to become savvy to the wiles of human nature. Vowing never to let her heart be stomped on again, she was now tough as nails. She hid her soft, vulnerable emotions behind her strong, physical prose.

Grace gently tugged on Francy's arm. "Girl, we better skedaddle before Castro blows our cover," she whispered. Grace turned to Manford Grove and gave a polite smile as she escorted Francy out to the docks.

Castro followed the girls outside. "I don't know what you two are up to, but you're not going to get away with it." Castro stuffed his paycheck in his back pocket and swung his sunglasses back onto his face.

"I can't believe you came back to work on the docks," Francy turned to Castro. "Even after the accident." Francy looked down at his feet. "Still wearing your signature boots?"

"These boots saved my life!"

"Accident?" Grace chimed in with her habitual curiosity.

"Yes," Francy confirmed. "A broken leg. That's why I talked him out of working on the docks and becoming a personal trainer at the gym."

"It seems like there are a lot of accidents happening here," Grace mugged. "Not my idea of a great work environment."

"Work at the gym can be unpredictable. There was an opportunity for a side hustle here on the docks, so I took it."

"It seems to me that you are good at taking a lot of opportunities," Francy quickly commented.

"Oh, yes," Grace said innocently, "how is Mrs. White doing?"

"I'm on to you and your whole group. I know what you did." Castro slicked back his dark hair, turned, and walked away.

Grace gave Francy a hug. "Girl, are you ok?"

Francy smiled. "Yes, I'm good. We just had a history. This was before I met you, Grace. Castro was the first guy I fell hard for."

"That's obvious," Grace whispered. "What did he mean by 'he's on to the whole group?'"

"He thinks Debra, along with all of us killed Ansel."

"Are you sure he wasn't hit on the head in that accident?" Grace rolled her eyes. "Hey look, here comes Drew."

"Girls, any luck?" Drew caught up with them by the side of the dock.

"We have some news for you," Francy smiled.

"Good, I do too." Drew was eager to share. "Come on, I'll tell you on the way."

"Where are we going?" Grace asked. She hiked up her skirt and ruffled it like a can-can dancer. "If it gets any hotter…"

"I talked to Israel. He's meeting us at Lincoln Road for lunch," Drew grinned. "We have some clues to unravel."

Israel's mind was going at a hundred knots per second. Hyper and vigilant, he was a superstar of multi-tasking. 20 errands and 10 phone calls in 15 minutes was the way he operated. "Now where did that flash drive go?" he questioned himself. Dodging between his eager dog Nina and his indolent cat, Titi, Israel popped the toast down in the toaster, hit the send button on his current email to his acting coach, and dug through his dirty laundry in a hot minute.

"Here you are. Hiding on me, eh?" Israel pulled out the flash drive from the pocket of his black tuxedo pants he wore the night of the funeral on the boat.

He ripped off his shirt and changed shoes. He quickly feed Nina and Titi, put on a clean shirt, grabbed his laptop from the kitchen counter, and opened his front door. He grabbed his scooter and the piece of toast that launched itself out of the toaster. "Ciao chicas!" he addressed the pets as he dashed out through the front door of his building.

———⊰✄⊱———

Lincoln Road was a beautiful esplanade running east to west from the Atlantic Ocean to the edge of Alton Road. Filled with high-end retail shops and a variety of outstanding restaurants, it was the perfect place to see and be seen. It's transition from a forest of mangroves in 1912 to its current state as one of the most magnificent outdoor malls in America, cemented its reputation as a place of tropical beauty and yet another iconic site in Miami's ever-changing landscape.

The dancers loved meeting at their favorite hot spot, Café Cubana. A local restaurant with a mix of tropical favorites and healthy food options, it was the perfect place to gather after class or when they would finish a late-night dance gig at one of the nightclubs.

"I only count six?" Daniel was their favorite waiter and always remembered what everyone liked.

"Israel's on his way," Drew smiled as Aisha and Debra gave him a big kiss hello.

"You work around all this delicious Cuban food and you still have such a great body," Aisha flirted with the waiter. "Mui guapo, papi."

Francy and Grace huddled at one end of the long table and shared what they had learned at the docks with Elena and the girls. Drew recapped what he had learned from his conversation with Walter.

Israel rolled up on his scooter. "Amigos." He bounced off his wheels and parked himself at the table between Francy and Drew. He opened his laptop and allowed it to boot up.

"So, this flash drive must have fallen out of Walter's pocket the night of his father's funeral on the boat. He must have lost it when he ran into you, Israel," Drew figured.

"Yeah, he was trying to make it to the side of the boat so that he wouldn't vomit all over the place," Israel recalled.

"It's funny, but I did not recognize the logo on the flash drive until I saw it again in a folder on Katie Roma's desk. Then, we saw it on the glass window of *White Lightning Shipping.*"

"I'm just going to run this for any viruses," Israel said as he stuck the flash drive into his laptop.

"Walter told me that Lizette, Falcon White's assistant had information pertaining to the flash drive that she was supposed to give to Ansel," Drew remembered.

The whole group watched as Israel brought up the information on the flash drive. "Ah, damn! It's an encrypted file," Israel exclaimed.

"What does that mean, exactly?" Grace had a perplexed look on her face.

"With an encrypted file, the data is translated into an unreadable format that can only be unscrambled with a password or decryption key," Israel explained.

"Then, Lizette has the encryption key. Maybe that's what she was supposed to give Ansel," Aisha surmised.

"Falcon White gave Walter the flash drive to hold on to at the docks, the night he was murdered. He was afraid it would fall into the wrong hands during his meeting," Drew assumed.

"But Walter claimed he didn't know what was on the file." Francy recollected.

"So, by giving Walter the flash drive and perhaps the encryption key to Ansel, it was to ensure that both of them had to be present to open it," Drew deduced.

"Or maybe it was to protect both of them," Grace added.

"I love how you think, Grace. That's that motherly instinct of yours."

"Well, it didn't protect Ansel." Debra said somberly.

Grace let the comment just roll off like water on a rain jacket. That was Grace's strength. As a dancer, there were always adverse comments and rejection to deal with and Grace had her coping skills down to a science.

"We're sorry, love" Aisha put her arm around Debra's shoulders. "We understand it's been a rollercoaster ride. But we are here for you."

"Did Detective Vincent have any more information about Ansel?" Israel asked.

Drew shook his head. "He asked me to come in and talk with him. I think the Miami police and detective squad are batting zero with both murders. He seems to think if we all put our heads together, something might make sense."

"I heard from Kyle, the White's lawyer. The reading of Falcon White's will be postponed since the death of Ansel," Israel added.

"You know the White's lawyer?" Elena asked.

"Sure, we all do. He takes Francy's classes."

"Drew, the jewel you found in Lizette's car, did it look familiar?" Elena enquired.

"Not really. It was teardrop shaped. It looked like it fell out of a setting. There were marks on the side of the stone that seemed to resemble prongs."

"Do you mind if I take it to an acquaintance of mine?" Elena asked. She recalled the nice sales associate at Tiffanys who helped her and Walter.

"That's a great idea, Elena."

Daniel came to the table with the group's usual drink orders. He had a look of hesitation on his face. He seemed pensive about something as both Aisha and Grace noticed the odd behavior of their trusted friend.

"Ok Daniel, spill the beans." Elena noticed as well. "You definitely can't hold onto a secret."

Daniel served the last drink and set down his tray. He slowly pulled out his phone and scrolled to a news alert notification that came across his screen just minutes earlier. He took his phone to Drew. Drew read it to the group, out loud:

"Sexy Seven face mounting questions after murder weapon is found in their possession."

"What?" Grace screeched. "What is that about?" she questioned, her hands shaking.

"None of us found a murder weapon, did we?" Francy asked.

Each dancer looked at one another, expecting a confession. Yet, none came. "What kind of malarkey is this?" Elena commented.

Drew asked Daniel when he got the news flash.

"It just came in," Daniel confessed.

"We are being set up!" Israel shouted.

"How could the press even print something like this? It's simply heresy" Debra added. "Should I call my attorney?"

"The press has made greater assumptions with less facts than this in the past." Drew shook his head in disbelief. "It doesn't surprise me. Someone has them in their back pocket."

"This puts us squarely in the spotlight and it's not good."

"I don't like this. We are in way over our heads." Francy confessed.

"This is a whole other level. We are now being accused of something we should not be involved in. Somebody has it out for us." Elena was now angry. She pulled back her pigtails and pinned them to the top of her head. "We have to get control of this."

"I think we're in for a real storm" Francy stood up, shaking the tension out of her body. "We have to go," she said, looking at her watch. "We have the studio scheduled for a dance rehearsal."

"Where are you performing? Daniel asked.

Drew handed the waiter back his phone. "We are performing at Wynwood, so we have to be flawless."

"Stay strong my friends," Daniel added with a solemn look on his face. "I'm rooting for you."

The gym was a fifteen-minute walk from Lincoln Road. The conversation was stifled by the accusation they were just accused of in the press. They walked into the dance studio with great in trepidation.

"It's weird that we have not been here, since…" Francy paused. She swallowed hard, almost as if she didn't want to say what everyone was thinking. On some level, Drew expected to see Ansel's body still hanging there.

"This is surreal," Elena added. Looking around, they noticed nothing out of place. The dance studio was spotless. It was if a gruesome murder was never unearthed there.

"Let's focus on the task at hand," Francy reminded them. She ran them through their routine. As performers, they were masters of synchronicity, each movement a mirror of the other, a seamless blend of rhythm and grace within the confines of the dance studio. Yet, when they stepped out into the harsh world of reality, beyond the safe boundaries of their rehearsed world, they found themselves confronted with a challenge of monumental proportions—a situation so rare and intense that few individuals would ever encounter it in the span of their lives.

"We look good," Francy told them after an hour of rehearsal. "Why don't we go home and try to get some rest before this evening."

Drew got home quickly. His mind was distracted with every detailed absurdity they were mixed up in. So many unanswered questions. So many angles that made no sense. He had lost sight of his day-to-day life chores. Laundry, food shopping, emails…

"I need to run some errands before heading over to Wynwood for the show this evening," Drew thought to himself. A quick shower and change of clothes were followed by switching shoes and collecting the Alo dance bag he only used for show days. He grabbed his bag and headed out the door.

Lost in thought, he was suddenly and keenly aware of a strong odor around him. When he realized where it was coming from, Drew opened his dance bag. The putrefying scent of blood caught him off guard. Fearful of what was sitting in waiting, he turned on the bright flashlight on his phone and dropped the bag to the curb. He cautiously pried open the string borders of the black satchel even further and peered inside, his heart racing.

Wrapped in a bloodied white handkerchief was a silver dagger approximately eight inches in length adorned with a white ivory handle and gilded with a silver tip at the top of the hilt. There was dried blood still encrusted along the upper edge of the sharp blade. Drew's heart dropped into his stomach. "What the hell?" he whispered to himself. He couldn't speak.

This looks very incriminating he thought. "What do I do?"

His first call was to Debra. "Meet me off of Lincoln Road at the New World Center in Bougainvillea Park in 30 minutes."

The New World Center was located one block north of Lincoln Road. A beautiful concert hall built to house Miami's New World Symphony; it was the crowned jewel of South Beach. Adorned by a half-acre of towering metal structures in the form of tornados, they encased gorgeous, paperesque bougainvillea flowers that grew up through the center of the frames dripping with their colorful pallets of burgundy and fuchsia.

Debra pulled her BMW up along the curb in front of the park and slowly made her way out of the car. She had been visibly crying. Losing her fiancé, being implicated in a murder, and almost being roadkill within a two-week span of time, was overburdening her senses. Drew's news was about to send her over the edge.

"I didn't know what to do?" Drew confessed after showing her the contents of his dance bag. He was now caught up in the same tears as Debra.

They sat under the dangling flower-scape holding each other. Debra gathered her repose. "How did that get in your bag?"

"I always leave my bag backstage during shows," Drew thought back.

"Yes, but where was the last place you had this bag? Think hard. Try to remember."

His mind was full of information that seemed to make no sense. He couldn't come up with an answer.

"We have just been implicated in having in our possession, the murder weapon," Debra spoke through her tears. "And it somehow materializes?" Debra's thoughts were also clouded in confusion and self-doubt. "Mi amor, I'm sorry. I'll only ask this once, but that's not your knife, is it?

"It was downtown at the nightclub where we performed last! I remember now. I only use this dance bag for shows," Drew recalled. "Of course, it's not mine. Anybody could have put that dagger in my bag. We were performing in a night club with over a thousand people."

"Well, we know Ansel was stabbed to death," Debra cried. She bent over gripping her stomach as if she could not handle one more thing. Her psychosomatic pain wrapped around her tender abdomen. It was so out of character for her. Debra realized it had taken its toll. She put her arms around Drew for consol.

"Oh, what are we going to do?" Debra sniffled. She took a beat and slowly rose. Short in stature, but tall in pride and self-confidence, she was not going to take it anymore. "We've got to get to the bottom of this," she demanded. "For some reason, we keep getting dragged further and further into this and we need to figure out why before we are the prime suspects in this mess. This must be the same knife that killed Ansel?" Debra had a look of determination on her face.

"Do you think that whole show Daphne put on that night in the VIP lounge was a sham?" Drew questioned.

"Did she kill her brother and then slip the knife into your bag?" Debra thought. And Walter? Where was he that night?"

"I'm sorry Debra," Drew observed.

"I really loved Ansel. He was a sweet man who adored me, I was looking forward to the fantasy of spending the rest of my life with him. We were going out for about six months, but I never expected an engagement proposal," she confided. "I think the death of his father accelerated his timeline to get engaged and thought that kind of stability would bring some normalcy to his already crazy life." Debra gathered her mixed thoughts and feelings spinning through her head.

They sat in silence.

It was as if they were frozen. Frozen from fear and helplessness.

"OK," Drew stood up. "Enough of feeling sorry for ourselves. We have to take back control." He offered Debra his hand. She grasped it and stood up, her eyes gazing into his with complete trust.

"I know that look," she said sternly.

"We need answers and I know just the expert who can help us." Drew was now determined. His posture changed. His mind found solace in his answer. We are going to the Ritz Carlton.

Debra looked at Drew with a perplexed look on her face.

"We know an expert who can help us," Drew confirmed.

A look of comprehension changed Debra's posture. "Of course, we have an expert in our corner. Maybe she can give us answers regarding this dagger and where it might have come from."

"Let's pay Deborah Desilets a visit," Drew concluded.

At the end of Lincoln Road, where the sand met the sea, stood the famous Ritz Carlton hotel. Deborah Desilets was Miami's premier architect and a purveyor of fine art who kept an office in the hotel.

Her association with the same architect who created Lincoln Road, the Fontainebleau Hotel, and the current Ritz Carlton, Morris Lapidus, was personal. As the last associate to the man behind Miami Beach's extraordinary revival in the Golden Years, Deborah Desilets held art and preservation at the top of her list. She was a force to be reckoned with.

Drew and Debra jumped in her BMW and headed over a few blocks. "I just texted her," Drew confirmed to Debra.

"Thank goodness she takes Francy's class," Debra smiled. "We have an in."

"She says come on up," Drew read her text back to Debra.

They valet parked at the Ritz and headed upstairs through the posh hotel.

"There's her office." Drew pointed.

"You're going to show her the knife?" Debra feared. "Blood and all?"

"Listen," Drew whispered. "She is very cool. She knows what time it is and she's very discreet. Why do you think she's gotten where she is today. She's a very savvy woman." Drew's words were somewhat comforting to Debra, who was now having second thoughts.

They stepped nervously into the chic, expansive gallery of Deborah Desilets. The walls were adorned with priceless art masterpieces, each with its own story and history. Despite the intimidating grandeur of the place, their focus was on the elegant woman who stood before them.

Deborah was a blond beauty of a certain age, a timeless vision of grace and charm. Her hair, the color of ripened wheat, cascaded over her shoulders, framing her expressive face. Her sky-blue eyes, full of intelligence and wit, sparkled under the gallery lights. Dressed in an elegant, form-fitting floral dress, she was a compelling mix of strength and femininity. Her age was hard to determine - she had the vitality of a young woman, yet her eyes held the wisdom of someone who had lived and loved deeply.

"I sensed the urgency in your text," Deborah smiled as she greeted the pair with hugs and kisses.

"Was it that obvious?" Drew frowned.

"Considering I got a news update over my phone about you guys being in possession of a murder weapon…" she glanced out her large windows at the calm sea. "I figured it must be something intriguing enough for you to reach out."

"We've been set up!" Debra interjected.

"No doubt," Deborah smiled warmly. "You're treading in dangerous waters with some dubious people." Deborah's brain was like a lock-box of information and little facts about Miami Beach, its culture, as well as its dubious past. It was this "past" that she found the most intriguing. Miami was built on the blood, sweat, and tears of those who came before. She knew a treasure trove of secrets, which she only unlocked when it was pertinent to do so.

Drew wanted to sit down in a plush velvet chair that was beside him, but he was too nervous. He paced instead. He slowly reached for his dance bag. His palms were sweating as he contemplated if his decision to visit Deborah was the right one. "I'm going to preface this by telling you I found this knife in my dance bag. It was placed in my bag sometime after Ansel White's murder."

Deborah listened to every word. She understood that she was being offered sensitive and possibly incriminating information. Therefore, she knew to handle it with the utmost discretion. Deborah sensed the fear that surrounded her friends. She would be honest, yet compassionate to the unfathomable situation Drew and his friends were coping with.

Drew gently pulled the weapon out of his bag. The knife was still wrapped in the handkerchief, the scent of iron and dampness permeated the air.

Deborah quickly slipped on a pair of rubber gloves she pulled from her desk drawer. "This is a magnificent piece," she said, her eyes studying the knife with a professional intensity. "It's an authentic Arabian knife, dating back to the 7th century. This type of knife was used by the Bedouin tribes of the Arabian Peninsula."

She went on to explain the knife's history, its unique design reflecting the rich Arabic culture of the time. The handle was made of camel bone, the blade of high carbon steel. "This arabesque design," she explained, "was not mere decoration but a symbolic representation of the Bedouin's nomadic lifestyle."

Deborah reached for a magnifying glass. Her eyes widened with interest as she picked up the ornate knife again. Her expert hands gently felt the curve of the handle, her fingers tracing the intricate designs etched on the blade and hilt.

"The knife," she said, "is a symbol of courage and survival, essential tools for the harsh desert life. It was also a status symbol, its intricate designs signifying the owner's wealth and social standing."

Drew and Debra looked at each other. "This is a collector's piece?" Debra asked.

As Deborah revealed the knife's history, Drew and Debra responded in awe. The knife they thought was an ordinary antique was, in reality, a priceless piece of history.

"The blood spatter was a violent consequence to the way it was used," she said, shaking her head. "Tell the police that you noticed blood in the hilt and that they must check this out." Deborah shook her head, without revealing her emotions.

"The police?" Debra questioned.

Deborah didn't react. She carefully wrapped the bloodied weapon back in its handkerchief and handed it to Drew.

Deborah then motioned for them to sit down.

"Did you have any connection to the family?" Drew asked, leaning back in the beautifully designed chair.

"Ahhh," Deborah sighed. "Well, before he had a family, Falcon White and I had a history. Her eyes softened as she spoke of him, her voice imbued with the memories of a past romance. She spoke of their relationship before he was married, a brief period when he was a young, charming, and ambitious man. Their love was passionate and fiery, yet it was not meant to last. Falcon had other plans, other dreams, and so, they went their separate ways.

"But today is not about lost love," she spoke in a half whisper. "It is about an antique knife that was used as a murder weapon and then found its way to you." She stood up and Drew and Debra followed. They knew that was their cue to go. They graciously thanked Deborah and left the office. "See you in class!" Deborah waved.

They left the gallery with a newfound appreciation for the Arabian culture and a deep respect for Deborah, the blond beauty with a past as intriguing as the art, architecture, and antiques she preserved.

"We've got bigger problems now." Drew was deep in thought. "I have to take this to Detective Vincent."

"What? Are you crazy? You might as well hang a noose around your neck!" Debra was enraged. "He's going to haul you right off to prison."

"Detective Vincent knows me a long time. We were buddies in New York when he was just a beat cop. He knows I'm not a murderer."

Debra sat down again, shaking her head. "Well, alright! But I'm coming with you!"

CHAPTER 9

WYNWOOD

ALL DETECTIVE VINCENT could do was shake his head. "You didn't touch it, did you?" He looked at Drew and Debra as if he was scolding school children.

"No sir, we did not," Drew replied.

"How did this end up in your possession?"

"Clearly, it was a plant!" Debra, ready to argue, raised one hand in the air in the motion of "obviously."

Drew and Debra preceded to fill Detective Vincent in on the information they had obtain from being around the White's associates and family members.

"I'm impressed with your detective work and the initiative it took to follow your instincts. All of you." Detective Vincent leaned over and picked up a very thick file from his desk. It had Falcon White's name on the side.

"We investigated the nightclub after you told me about the meeting with you and Daphne White. We found the main crime scene where Ansel was killed behind the club. There were large pools of blood and signs of struggle." Detective Vincent flipped through the pages of the folder. "There was also a partial shoe print we found." Detective Vincent looked at Debra. He imagined that it must have been hard for her to hear this information. "Debra, again, I'm sorry for your loss."

Debra nodded her head.

Detective Vincent continued to flip through the folder. He came to an autopsy report on Ansel. "There was trace material found on the back of his legs and in his shoes, which turned out to be coral stone. This was not found anywhere near the club. The coroner confirms he was killed with a blade about eight inches in length. Looking at the blade you brought me, it appears to be the same length."

"But why plant it in my bag?" Drew questioned.

"Probably because the killer was either trying to hide it or trying to frame you for the murder," Detective Vincent confirmed.

"How did the press know about this before we did?" Drew was confused.

"The perpetrator must have leaked this information to the press. When there was no buzz about you and the blade being picked up by the police after the murder, they must have leaked this information. The news media loves sensationalism. They barely fact-check anymore. They quickly put the story out there, hoping to have the exclusive." Detective Vincent had seen this many times before. "This kind of press creates suspicion making any case difficult to send to trial with an unbiased filter. It's my guess the killer wants to blame you for the murder of Ansel White."

"Mrs. White and that buffoon of a boyfriend already attempted to accuse us of killing Ansel." Debra added.

"Two family members dead and we have not made much progress. We have interviewed the family. We have talked to the workers at the docks. We have interrogated known associates." Detective Vincent haphazardly twirled a pencil around his fingers. "We have several clues and circumstantial evidence, yet no solid leads. I'm just stumped."

"Well, we have to go," Debra interjected. "We have a show in Wynwood."

"I want both of you and your group to be careful. You were just accused in the press with possession of the murder weapon, so people are going to be on the defensive. Be aware!" Detective Vincent wanted to convince them not to go, but he knew Drew was determined and his friends would always trust his judgement.

North of Downtown Miami in the greater Miami neighborhood called Wynwood, there once was a collection of warehouses which were transformed in recent years into one of the world's hippest hangouts. Full of eclectic restaurants, bars and shops, Wynwood also offered visitors countless opportunities to enjoy the best of international contemporary art, whether in galleries or simply on the street. The surrounding areas were now converted warehouses housing craft breweries and funky art galleries. A hip young crowd frequented the neighborhood's chic clothing boutiques, stylish bistros, and late-night bars. Non-stop energy and in-the-moment style were the hallmarks of Wynwood.

Within Miami's newfound artistic haven, the Wynwood Walls were captivating murals displaying an incredible fusion of inventive brilliance and urban sophistication. This stylish open-air gallery had quickly become a hub for the avant-garde.

As throngs of visitors mingled, savoring cocktails and exploring a rich tapestry of striking sculptures, vibrant frescoes, and provocative art installations, DJ Carga's ambient music enveloped them in a comfortable yet invigorating atmosphere.

Suddenly, a young girl's shriek pierced the air from a distant corner of the courtyard. She had been admiring a sculpture that unexpectedly came to life. Onlookers watched in awe as Israel and Aisha, clad in painted leotards and skullcaps, began dancing to the pulsating bass reverberating off the walls.

Another astonished cry erupted from across the courtyard when Drew, Francy, and Debra seemed to emerge from a vivid mural they previously blended into.

Grace and Elena appeared from behind another wall, dressed in half black and half white leotards, resembling the ends of the picture's frame. The group standing next to them gasped, not expecting the frame to come to life.

The performers congregated at the courtyard's center, striking a pose reminiscent of a Picasso masterpiece. As Francy led her dancers through an extraordinary performance throughout the art installations, onlookers flocked to witness their hypnotic display. The rhythmic music filled the space as spectators became spellbound by the dancers' electrifying moves.

"That's them. They're here," a girl in the audience shouted out.

From his vantage point, Drew saw several people gasp and point. As he moved through the choreography, he watched people's reactions roll across the courtyard like a rogue wave.

"It's the murders." Israel was in earshot of another audience member's comment. He nudged Debra who was next to him. She ignored it, just hoping the sentiment would pass.

It passed through the crowd like a wildfire. Now, there was distinct rumbling as the crowd stirred. DJ Carga noticed the change in the atmosphere. She turned the music up.

The dancers turned simultaneously, moving from center stage to a group of onlookers standing stage right. "Yeah!" The group cheered raising their hands in approval. "We love you guys," a fan yelled out.

It quickly became evident that there were two distinct factions, each harboring contrasting opinions about the performers. Thanks to the recent headline, half of the crowd firmly believed that the dancers were not as innocent as they appeared, with some even suspecting them of the heinous crimes Miami could not stop talking about.

Camera phones were all up, recording their every move as the dancers swept across the stage, catching crowd reactions from one end of the performance space to the other.

As emotions flared and verbal opinions started to clash, the crowd became louder and more opinionated, engulfed in a fierce rivalry, each side trying to convince the other of their unwavering stance.

"Aisha, over here!" The press had arrived. Pushing their way into the small space already packed with spectators, cameras flashed as reporters seemed to emerge from out of nowhere.

Heated debates filled the air, with voices rising and merging into a maelstrom of arguments and shouting matches. DJ Carga tried turning up the music even higher to drown out the mayhem.

Aisha's keen eye caught sight of Joyce White, disguised in the crowd. Aisha passed by Drew on stage, making sure he was aware of Joyce's presence.

"Look to your left," Drew whispered, "Daphne's next to her."

Meanwhile, amongst the fervor of this engrossing spectacle, Joyce White and her daughter Daphne found themselves caught in the midst of the swirling crowd.

Together, mother and daughter maneuvered through the spectators, listening intently to the impassioned arguments echoing back and forth in the audience. Determined to watch the explosive interactions of the opinionated crowd, they made their way through the throngs of protestors, observing their reaction to the dancers.

Shocked by their reception, the dancers moved through their routine, fearful of what the rioting crowd would do next. Francy's words echoed in Drew's head. She was right. They had walked into a storm.

It was now an all-out riot. The dancers broke character and quickly scattered behind the walls. A girl in the crowd grabbed Drew's arm as he was trying to make his escape. "Call me," she said, flicking her hair to one side. She stuffed a paper in his hand.

Drew, startled by the girl's quick action, didn't respond and followed the others through the vivid artwork behind the wall and down a path that took them out to a side street, where they jutted to safety.

"What is happening?" Grace cried, deeply out of breath as Drew helped her into Israel's car.

"We have to get out of here," Israel shouted as he stepped on the gas.

Debra threw her hands up in the air and shook them at the Universe. "What next?"

"I just knew that was coming," Francy said wiping the sweat off her brow.

"I could only think of your words during the performance," Drew confirmed. "We've already been accused in the court of public opinion."

"Well, not everyone thought so," Elena added. "We are heroes to some."

Aisha cleared her throat. "Did everyone see Joyce and Daphne in the crowd?"

"They probably started the riot," Israel responded.

"I don't know about that," Drew thought out loud.

"They could have been skewered by half that crowd too," Elena reassured. "Some people think they are the guilty party."

"Except they were in disguise," Aisha exclaimed, "hiding under those hoodies and sweatpants."

"We have to lay low for a little while," Francy suggested. "We are bringing on too much heat! I'm going to cancel our next few performances."

"Then we are just going to look guilty," Aisha pressed. "We might want to rethink that idea."

"Don't forget, we have the funeral tomorrow," Debra reminded everyone.

"And who invited us to this invitation only event?" Israel inquired as they turned onto the highway to the beach.

"Lizette." Elena said pushing her blond hair aside as she pulled her skull cap off her head. "She insisted we come. She said we were there for Falcon's funeral on the boat and Ansel and Debra were engaged. Lizette thought it was the right thing to do."

"Or she's setting us up for another ambush," Drew surmised. He reached down and pulled the piece of paper out of his pocket that the girl in the crowd gave him.

"More admiring fans?" Aisha smirked.

"Elena, did Lizette hand-write that invitation?" Drew's face lit up as he looked at the girl's note.

Elena thought back for a moment. "No, it was a printed invitation."

"These people and their invitations..." Debra huffed.

"No wait." Elena recalled. "She did sign it. And left her phone number for the RSVP."

"We need to look at that invitation. I have an idea!"

CHAPTER 10

MIAMI CITY CEMETERY

***

THE CAW OF the crows echoed off the cold stoned epitaphs. A solemn contrast to the bright and sunny Miami morning. The Miami City Cemetery was the oldest and most famous cemetery. It was the final resting place for generations of families from a bygone era. And now she was accepting two more of its residents into the heart of her bosom.

The atmosphere was heavy with grief, tinged with a sense of unease. The father and son's tragic deaths had shaken the community and whisper of a mysterious murderer was the most prominent gossip circulating the city.

Security for the funeral was tight. A large perimeter was established in the vicinity of the mausoleum in order to ensure safety and privacy for the family. The guests started lining up for the service before sunrise. A configuration of mourners snaked through the gates, reaching the established perimeter where they had to produce the funeral invitation and walk through a metal detector.

Aisha and Grace glided secretly through the crowd, their black shrouds and long dresses exuding an air of mystery. Francy and Elena, also cleverly disguised in black tulle, quietly converged, unknowingly from different directions behind Walter, Daphne, and Joyce.

Elena watched Walter's expressions, trying to determine what was going through his mind. He would bite his lip precariously, then shove his hands in his pockets. She observed his eyes darting back and forth from his sister to his mother. She witnessed this all under the guise of her black funeral veil, strategically draped across her face.

Francy moved her gaze between the antsy crowd, standing uncomfortably in the heat and Lizette, who, for once, was standing as still as one of the marble angels guarding the grave next to her.

Grace had her eyes on Joyce White. This wife and mother lost a husband she distained and a son she adored in the span of a week's time. Yet, she appeared without emotion. No doubt, numb from the constant barrage of press, the relentless range of opinions, and the feeling of always being under a microscope. "Ahhh fame," Grace whispered to herself. She caught a glimpse of Detective Vincent and his men walking the perimeter of the burial site.

On the ridge above, curious onlookers and a throng of press were eagerly hoping for a glimpse of the family or any potential suspect gathered at the gravesite beyond.

As the eulogy and prayers unfolded, the dancers discreetly observed every person present. The mournful crowd was a diverse mix of close friends, family members, and unknown acquaintances. Drew couldn't help but wonder if the killer lurked amidst this multitude, blending seamlessly with the grieving masses. He had a very deep sense of anguish envelop him.

The invited guests were there for the internment, but they were also there for the spectacle. The heat bared down on the bereaved as curious eyes darted back and forth. The crowd could not seem to stay still. They shifted back and forth with an uneasiness that was visceral.

"Husband and father, Falcon White, and his son Ansel have found their eternal resting place," confirmed the priest. The massive crowd looked up from their prayers as he sprinkled holy water over two majestic gold and gilded urns perched atop a marble pedestal. Their silhouettes lingering beneath three towering palmetto trees, which symbolized peace and eternal life. The family mausoleum, which had stood there for over a century, loomed in the background.

Draped in black with a delicate lace shroud over her head, Debra wiped away tears, her cheeks gently caressed. Her body trembled as Drew stood by her side on the left and Israel on her right, providing unwavering support. Their identities hidden under tall top hats with black funerary veils cloaking their faces. Israel squeezed Debra's arm, offering comfort to quell her trembling.

In an instance, the peaceful silence was shattered. Suddenly, without warning, the ground beneath the mausoleum began to rumble and with an ear-splitting explosion, it burst open.

Dust and debris filled the air with a musty, gray matter. The ash and cinder cloud expanded upwards and outwards, propelling through the fearful mourners who were now scattering in every direction. Other guests screamed as projectiles from the blast spewed past them.

Detective Vincent immediately sprang into action. He quickly ordered his men to restore peace among the chaos. Some officers helped injured bystanders while others managed a perimeter in order to contain the scene.

Joyce, Daphne, and Walter White found themselves shielded from most of the explosion by the collapsing tarp that had protected them from the sun.

Israel and Drew's instincts kicked in as they quickly dove over Debra, protecting her from the flying debris.

Francy, Elena, and Grace darted in different directions, joining the parting crowd as terrified masses ran screaming from the horrifying scene.

Pandemonium spread across the cemetery. The press seized the moment and broke through the barricades, scrambling to capture the unexpected event. Cameras flashed, brightening the chaotic scene unfolding before them. Onlookers behind the barricades gasped in disbelief.

"It wasn't just the explosion that sent chills down their spines; it was yet another mysterious assault on Miami's famous family," expressed one reporter who was now streaming live on the radio.

"Whispers spread like wildfire among those who witnessed the spectacle. This had to be another sign from the killer or killers. A chilling message meant to haunt the White family further." Another reporter was already filming the live events for local television.

A barrage of press surrounded the White family. The reporters delved deeper, yelling out questions, interrogating the family members at their most vulnerable moment. The chaos made it seem like the opportune moment for reporters to bring up long-buried secrets and connect the dots between the explosion and the series of mysterious deaths that had Miami locked in fear.

"Who could have orchestrated this macabre display?" one reporter yelled out to Joyce White.

"Hey, Walter," another member of the press interjected, "you were an explosives expert in the Navy, weren't you? Weren't you injured from an explosion?"

Joyce looked at her son. Walter grabbed his leg involuntarily. He slowly looked up. His eyes scanned the crowd. He turned away from the reporter who was expecting a defensive response.

"It's rumored that a murder weapon was found in the possession of the Sexy Seven," a reporter squealed. "Can you confirm this?" The press became more determined than ever to uncover the truth. Again, there was no response.

Drew heard the question but stayed concealed under his top hat and long veil, hiding his face. "Where is Aisha?" he wondered. He hadn't seen her since the explosion.

"Leave us alone!" Daphne screamed at the invading journalist as she ran to help the priest lying on the ground with a head wound. Beside him lay the shattered pieces of urns of Falcon and Ansel White. Their cremated remains were now a part of the aftermath. The exposed grave seemed like a gateway into the past. Black smoke poured from its center, shrouding the moment with even greater uncertainty. Around the gaping hole in the mausoleum lay chunks of ancient brick and mortar.

Several ambulances arrived as paramedics swiftly attended to the injured priest and others who suffered bruises and gashes from the cement shrapnel that had exploded outwards from the crypt.

Two SWAT vehicles pulled up alongside the disorderly crowd. The backdoors burst open, and two teams split up. One group secured the surrounding area. The other group wrangled Joyce, Walter, and Daphne into the van for protection.

The reporters were now looking for someone to interrogate and Lizette, Katie, and Castro became their next targets.

Before they could pounce on the unsuspecting trio, Detective Vincent and several of his men secured them from the infringing inquisitors and got them safely to the SWAT van.

Aisha peered out from behind the adjacent mausoleum. She discreetly observed the family position themselves beside their respective partners; Castro with Joyce, Katie with Daphne, and Lizette joining Walter. The family members and friends solemnly huddled together, their fractured peace trying to find some sense of normalcy amongst the chaos.

"Was Lizette really the mastermind behind this attack?" Aisha asked herself. She couldn't help but recall Drew's words from the day before.

Drew, Debra, and Israel quickly slipped out of sight behind a large columbarium. "Is everyone OK," Israel asked, breathing heavy.

"This is just ghastly!" Debra exclaimed.

"Has anyone seen Aisha?"

"You're practically in the sightline of the press." Aisha stepped out from behind them. "We should split up and head for the front gate because the press, as well as our condemning public might spot us lurking here together."

They dashed in four directions for the front gate of the cemetery.

The following morning, the dancers woke up together after seeking refuge in Israel's apartment. Drew couldn't sleep and spent the night talking with Elena and Debra, who also dared not fall asleep in fears that their reality would become part of their nightmares.

Francy and Israel were already up, playing video games on Israel's Nintendo as a form of distraction. Their competitive natures kept them from thinking about the horrors they had also endured.

Grace and Aisha were in the kitchen, preparing breakfast. "Food is a great distraction," Grace announced as she served the group her famous eggs benedict.

"And don't forget a side of "*Revenge!*" This was Aisha's creation. A shot of vodka, tequila, light rum, triple sec, gin with a splash of grenadine. "I make sure they serve this at all my wrap parties after we finish a film," the movie actress confirmed.

"It must be brunch already. I'll drink to that." Elena was the first to grab a glass.

"Trust me," Aisha assured, "this brunch cocktail goes great with eggs benedict and a side of angst."

"What did we just experience?" Debra stood up, shaking her head.

"I don't know, but we have stepped squarely in the middle of it and we have to clear our names," Francy exclaimed as she grabbed a glass of *Revenge*. Our livelihood as dancers is in jeopardy."

"Ya, not to mention our lives," Israel chimed in.

"This is serious…" Debra reiterated. "We could have been blown up yesterday."

"Or molested by the press," Elena added, gulping her *Revenge*. All of a sudden, the look on Elena's face changed.

"Drew," Elena called out, looking up from her blinging phone. "It's Walter."

Drew stopped what he was doing and look across the room to see a look of concern on her face. "Elena, what is it?"

"It's Walter."

"What's Walter?" Drew looked perplexed, as he tried to read her expression.

"It's Walter. He has text me five times. He said, "It's urgent. Need to talk.""

"Call him." Grace called out from the kitchen.

"Don't call him!" Aisha interrupted.

"He wants me to come by the mansion," Elena starred at the text. "Drew, what should I do?"

Drew stopped to contemplate the big picture. What could be so urgent that he needed to talk to the one connection he had to the group, whom he trusted?

"Maybe he wants to confess?" Francy looked at Elena. "What do you think?"

"Maybe he wants to confess his undying love for you." Israel smirked.

"Elena, he obviously trusts you enough to reach out. How do you feel about going? Are you up for it?" Drew stood up and walked over to her. Elena seemed confused as she too was running scenarios through her mind.

"It could be a trap," Grace yelled from the kitchen.

"Well, I think I should go," she said hesitantly. "Let me text him back."

Out of curiosity, Drew walked over to the table and picked up his phone. "Detective Vincent has been texting me since the early morning. I had my phone on silence," Drew said cryptically looking down at the messages. "Something is going on."

"What's that?" Grace inquired.

"I had a hunch when we were in Wynwood. When we were running from that mob scene, a girl handed me a piece of paper. It made me think about Ansel's crime scene. We need to take a look at the note that was found on Ansel's body the morning we found him. Elena, do you still have that invitation from the funeral?"

"He just text me back. He asked me if I could come by now." Elena could feel the apprehension crawling up her spine. "Oh yes, hang on. Let me check and see if I still have that invite." Elena rifled through her purse and found the crumbled paper. "Here it is."

"OK, Elena, you head over to the White mansion. Debra, Israel, and Francy are going with me to see Detective Vincent."

"I'm tailing Elena in my car," Aisha confirmed. "You are not going alone."

"What do I do?" Grace added eagerly.

"Stay here!" everyone responded simultaneously.

Elena and Aisha took their separate cars and headed for the White mansion in Coconut Grove.

As they pulled into the circular drive of the White's family home, there was a line of police cars in the front of the sprawling grounds. The girls jumped out of their cars only to find Walter being led out in handcuffs from his private bungalow in the back of the property.

"I'm not the bad guy here." The girls could hear Walter vehemently maintain his innocence to his police escort. They watched in shock as two policemen led him down the circular drive and situated him in the back of the squad car, pushing his head down and into the vehicle before slamming the door.

Aisha noticed Joyce and Daphne looking out of the large Bay window in the front of the mansion, almost expressionless as Walter's fate seemed sealed.

Elena's cell phone rang. "It's Drew," she told Aisha.

"Elena, the police have a warrant to search Walter's bungalow and workshop. The police claim to have found compelling evidence linking Walter to the explosion."

"Did Detective Vincent share this compelling evidence?"

"Yes, we are here with him now," Drew explained. "They discovered traces of explosive material and detonators in Walter's workshop."

Elena froze. "How can that be?" she questioned.

"When we were at the cemetery, I overheard a reporter ask Walter about being an explosives expert in the Navy," Drew relayed to Elena.

"Yes, Walter had told me that he was a former Navy officer. He never mentioned being an explosives expert. I can see how that could raise immediate suspicions."

"Additionally," Drew went on, "the police uncovered a series of blueprints. Blueprints that seemed to be meticulous drawings of the cemetery and in particular, the White's Mausoleum."

Elena seemed discouraged. "Ok, we are heading to you!"

CHAPTER 11
STAR ISLAND

KYLE GENE, ESQUIRE, Miami's most famous lawyer, dancer, and head-turner, was known for his innocent baby face contrasted by his fierce and unrelentless determination. He was often compared to a vicious pit bull with a Cheshire cat's grin, ready to take on any legal challenge.

With his impressive track record, Kyle had earned the trust of the rich and famous, who sought his expertise in navigating the legal issues that came with wealth and fame. His unique problem-solving skills set him apart from other lawyers, making him a go-to-choice for complex and high-profile cases.

His firm's prestigious location, in the Brickell neighborhood of downtown Miami, reflected its commitment to serving the needs of wealthy individuals and prominent figures. Kyle's distinguished law firm was strategically paired with his stunning home on Star Island in order to establish his leverage as the island's elite lawyer. This positioned him with the reputation to attract high-net-worth clients.

"Detective Vincent, I'm here for my client, Walter White," Kyle shook Detective Vincent's hand.

Friends for years, Miami's top detective and The Sun City's top attorney shared mutual respect for each other. Often finding themselves on different sides of the proverbial coin, they knew how to work around each other and stay out of each other's way when need be.

"He was brought in for interrogation," Detective Vincent shared.

"Well, I am obligated to be there," Kyle reassured his friend.

Detective Vincent did his due diligence and lead Kyle to the room they were keeping Walter in. He then traversed to another room where Debra, Israel, Drew and Francy were waiting. Detective Vincent retrieved the note found on Ansel White's body from the evidence locker. "We determined that the phone number on the note was confirmed as Debra's cellphone. Ansel intended to text her when he arrived to pick her up that night at the club."

Debra nodded, her mind returning to that fateful evening.

"We were unable to establish the meaning of the additional set of numbers written below her phone number," Detective Vincent confirmed.

"Francy, do you have the invitation to the funeral?" Drew asked eagerly.

She pulled out the worn trifold invite from her dance bag that Elena had given her and handed it to Drew, unsure of what he was deducing.

"It's evident that two different people wrote on this paper. We know that Ansel wrote Debra's phone number." Drew looked at Debra, who nodded in agreement.

"It's clear that another person wrote the other number. Take a look at the loop of the 9 and the 3, present in both Debra's phone number and the unidentified numbers below. Note how Debra's number is slanted while the unknown set is not." Drew meticulously ensured that every detail was observed by everyone present.

Drew placed Ansel's note beside the funeral invitation. "At the bottom of this invitation is a handwritten portion that was inscribed by Lizette Brown. Notice the striking similarity in the handwriting. Four out of ten numbers on the funeral RSVP matched those in the unidentified set on Ansel's paper."

Detective Vincent reached into his desk and pulled out a magnifying glass. He observed the similarities under the loop.

"Lizette claims she had information she had to give to Ansel. Information that Falcon White wanted Ansel to have." Drew's mind tried unraveled the puzzle as he spoke the words. "This could be the key code to the flash drive."

Drew quickly explained to Detective Vincent that they had found a flash drive on the night of Falcon White's celebration on the boat.

"Ahhh, so you were withholding evidence?" Detective Vincent raised an eyebrow.

"No," Drew assured him. "We had no idea what it was or that it was even related. Israel, being the tech-savvy person he is, thought he could use the flash drive for storage and so he put it in his pocket after an accident on the boat."

"Do you think this could unlock the flash drive?" Detective Vincent inquired.

"It wasn't until Grace, Francy, and I had lunch with Katie Roma that I realized the logo on the flash drive matched the logo of the White's shipping business."

"So, you attempted to open the flash drive and discovered it was encrypted?" Detective Vincent summarized.

Suddenly, there was a knock at the door. A police officer opened it with Kyle standing behind him.

"Francy!" Kyle exclaimed. "I didn't expect to see you here. Look, the gangs all here."

Everyone stood up to greet Kyle.

"You know each other?" Detective Vincent was surprised.

"Kyle comes to Francy's class religiously to dance and get in a good workout," Israel interrupted. "His dancing is as stealth as his approach to the law. Precise and regimented."

"Does all of Miami take Francy's class?" Detective Vincent was still surprised.

"We've all known each other for so long, I forget that you are Miami's number one high-powered lawyer to the rich and famous," Francy complimented Kyle. "I just think of you as one of the gang."

"He'll always be a part of our gang." Israel smiled.

"Well, I hate to change the subject, but Detective Vincent, you can't hold my client. Your second-in-command has asked him all the questions I would allow and the evidence you have is circumstantial at best," Kyle confirmed.

"And how did you seemingly come to that conclusion?" Detective Vincent stared at Kyle as if he was crazy.

"Firstly, my client was an explosive expert in the Navy. True.

An expert, which means that poor excuse of a bomb that went off in the cemetery was not the work of an expert."

"Yes, SWAT determined it was crudely rigged, but that does not mean, he couldn't have done it," Detective Vincent argued. "Furthermore, the detonators recovered in my client's workshop were acquired from his Navy days as souvenirs." Kyle spun a chair around and sat, straddling its seat. "My client maintains that he had long lost interest in such matters and claimed he never had any intention of using them unlawfully."

"Heresy," Detective Vincent interrupted. "And...?"

Everyone one stared at Kyle with intent. The dancers had never heard their friend spin his magic as a high-powered lawyer.

"In regards to the blueprint of the mausoleum..." Kyle paused, dramatically. "Upon the death of his father, my client was considering expanding the family crypt. He received a copy of the blueprints from the cemetery right after his father's untimely demise. And..." he paused again, "my client had an alibi at the time of his father's death."

Detective Vincent was thumbing through the White's file. "Yes, I see there was an eye witness who put Walter in the car, waiting for his father, the night of his death. It doesn't mean he was not involved."

Kyle cleared his throat. "He has an alibi for his brother's death, as well. He was working late night in the docking office. Security at the docks have a record of this."

Detective Vincent was fast looking through the family files from earlier interviews they had conducted to confirm Kyle's story. Kyle paused and smiled revealing that large Cheshire cat grin.

Detective Vincent was speechless.

"Now, allow me to appeal to your sense of reason. There is no way my client could have done this." Kyle stood up. He motioned to Detective Vincent to join him outside. The two men stepped out.

There was dead silence in the room. The dancers looked at one another, not knowing what to say. Israel stood up and pointed to the door. They listened intently as they could hear Kyle's closing argument.

"My client, being the renowned bomb expert that he was, had his fair share of enemies who were well aware of his capabilities. Someone with malicious intent has deliberately framed him by utilizing his knowledge to shift the blame. You have no fingerprints, a timeline that doesn't add up, and no other reasons to hold my client. I'm sorry old friend, but all you have is circumstantial evidence." Kyle concluded.

Clearly disappointed, Detective Vincent unwittingly concurred and motioned to the accompanying officer to release Walter White. He quickly accompanied the officer to make sure the protocol was done correctly.

Kyle turned and stepped back into the room.

"So, tomorrow is the big day?" Drew asked Kyle.

"Yes, the reading of Falcon White's will. We were able to get the state of Florida to postpone the reading of the will due to the sudden death of his son, Ansel. But tomorrow is the day," Kyle confirmed.

"I wish I could be a fly on that wall," Israel joked.

"I'm sure you will hear about the outcome in the news. People are not discreet in this family," Kyle smirked. "Hey, I don't know what you are going to do about the crowd downstairs?

Israel's face changed to a more serious look.

"There are reporters and a huge crowd waiting for your group outside. Half of Miami wants to blame you guys for the White's deaths, while the other half see you all as heroes. There are fans chanting your names," Kyle said in disbelief.

"Detective Vincent has gotten us a security detail. He also thinks if we stick together, it would be easier to protect us as one unit. It's crazy!" Israel shook his head.

"Well Elena and Aisha are not coming up here," Drew confirmed, silencing his cell phone. "They saw the crowd downstairs and diverted to Aisha's place."

Detective Vincent entered the room. "Kyle, we have secured your client and will take you both out of here in a squad car, as you will never get through the crowd outside."

The dancers stood up. "What do we do?" Drew asked.

"Israel and I are going to his apartment to look at the flash drive. Maybe we have the code to unlock it, thanks to you guys," Detective Vincent smiled. "I want the rest of you to sit tight. Drew, let me talk to you in private, please?"

Drew shot Francy and Debra a look, trying to determine what he wanted to say in private.

Detective Vincent turned to the nearest police officer. "Send a car to the White mansion again. We need to bring in Lizette Brown."

The two stepped out of the room.

"Drew, I can see the look of disappointment on your face. I know you are thinking this case could end up like your aunt's case... cold and unsolved, but I assure you, we will get to the bottom of this. We will solve this case."

Drew's mind immediately went back to California where he experienced the murder of his favorite aunt, in his late teens. He always felt responsible because he imagined he could have tried to solve what the police could not. Now, 25 years later, being thrown into a similar situation, he was even more frustrated as they seemed to take two steps forward and three steps back.

"Stay positive. I know things seem bleak, but we'll catch a break."

Drew smiled, politely as Detective Vincent knew exactly what Drew was thinking. "I suppose that's what drives you," He surmised.

Drew suddenly discerned the connection. There was a curiosity; a drive, even. A drive to unearth the mystery. A passion to unfurl the truth and find closure. If not for himself, for the ones who were hurting. Hurting like he was.

"Your police escort is here. We'll take you guys out the back gate," Detective Vincent assured.

The following day, Kyle arranged to have the White family gather in his home, for security purposes. Star Island was known for its luxurious homes, celebrity residents, and stunning waterfront views. It was also known for its assured protection. Situated on Biscayne Bay, this exclusive island was home to some of the most affluent individuals in the world.

The atmosphere inside Kyle's home was an elegant modern-tropical style with sheer linen curtains draped over large glass windows, looking east over the bay. Amidst that light and airy atmosphere entered the heavy anticipation that was the White family gathering for the enigmatic reading of Falcon White's will. The air seemed to crackle with anticipation as each member of the family, including wife Joyce, son Walter, daughter Daphne, girlfriend to Daphne, Katie Roma, and boyfriend to Joyce White, Castro Pryorr, took their place in the sun-lit room. Falcon White's assistant, Lizette Brown was strangely absent.

Muffled whispers passed between them, unsure of what to expect. Without the presence of their belated Ansel, the tension was high. The police had investigated the family's motives, the press appeared to scrutinize their every move, and the city's very public perception of them added an eerie undertone to the proceedings. As Kyle entered the room, a hush fell over the gathering, and all eyes turned to him, eager to learn the secrets that the will would unveil.

The lawyer's voice was solemn and measured as he began recounting the life and accomplishments of Falcon White. "We are gathered here today to read the last will and testament of Falcon White. The document was written three years before without changes," Kyle confirmed. "The original was filed in the Miami courthouse, and I hold a copy of it here."

Kyle cleared his throat. "The will was witnessed by your banker, Mr. Suarez of the Miami Central Bank. There were no changes made to the will after the death of Ansel White. This is still the original will. I preface the reading of this will with these remarks to prepare you for its contents."

The family exchanged looks, unsure as to what Kyle was referring to.

Kyle continued. *"I, Falcon J. White. being of sound mind and body, do hereby declare this to be my last will and testament, prepared by my own hand and legally witnessed."*

Kyle described Falcon White's achievements in the shipping business, his extraordinary wealth, and his remarkable family, as stated in the will. Tears rolled down Joyce White's eyes. Daphne, completely disinterested, sat there filing her nails. The remaining members of the group, shifted uneasy in their chairs, tension heightening with each passing word.

"I have bequeathed the entire inheritance and control of the flourishing shipping empire to my beloved daughter, Daphne White. Checkmate."

Gasps of disbelief rippled through the room, and astonished expressions appeared on the faces of the family. The revelation was met with a mixture of awe, envy, and suspicion, as the gravity of the situation sank in.

Daphne looked up from her nails in complete shock. Her disbelief was palpable. Katie Roma leaned into her and gave her a big hug. "I never lost hope, my darling," Katie whispered.

In that pivotal moment, the aura of mystery deepened, enveloping the room in an almost heavy cloak. Now, as they grappled with the unexpected turn of events, there was a sudden shift in the power dynamics. The enigmatic motive behind Falcon's decision and the implications of Daphne's newfound role all hung in the air.

"This just can't be," Daphne spoke for the first time.

Castro stood up and pointed his finger at Daphne. "You hated your father!" he yelled. "You don't even care for the business. We are going to fight this, aren't we Joyce?"

Joyce White sat in her chair, sobbing uncontrollably. Her life decisions and rollercoaster emotions centering around her husband -bubbled to the surface. Had she made wrong choices within their marriage? Had she given up on Falcon too soon? Was she moving in the right direction? Now, with no money, what was she to do? She didn't respond to Castro.

Castro turned to Kyle. "How do we fix this thing?"

Kyle, being the artful articulator, turned to Castro and said, "We will have to see about that." His innocuous answer seemed to calm Castro down, just enough to extinguish his rage and escort him and the rest of the family out of his home.

Daphne slowly rose from her chair as if she was not in control of her body. She walked over to Kyle and whispered, "Is this really true?"

Kyle confirmed the fact that she was the sole inheritor. "You know Daphne," he whispered to her, "chess enthusiasts experience unparalleled excitement at the possibility of sacrificing the queen, which is the strongest piece on the board." Kyle knew of the cat-and-mouse game Falcon wittingly played with his daughter. "It's inherently satisfying to sacrifice the queen to checkmate the enemy king."

She gave him a big kiss on the lips as she looked up to heaven. "You've won, father. Checkmate!"

The White family left the lawyer's home, each lost in their own thoughts. The once familiar ground had become a labyrinth of intricate puzzles and unanswered questions. The story of the reading of Falcon White's will became headline news, casting a spell of curiosity and leaving everyone eagerly awaiting the next chapter in the unfolding saga of the White family's legacy.

Several days after the press revealed to the world that Daphne White was now in charge of *White Lightning Shipping*, Daphne was reeling from her newfound quilt and sadness over the death of her father. Daphne made no public statements or appearances since that game-changing day. She finally realized her father loved her, only he didn't know how to express it. Since the death of her brother, she simply numbed her feelings and chose not to deal with them.

The news of the inheritance had overshadowed the murder mystery. Drew and his friends had no more performances scheduled after Wynwood. It was too dangerous to be seen in public or to put themselves out there in the spotlight for fear of retaliation.

Drew had no capacity to understand the totality of the situation. His friends were even worse off. They could not see how they were being branded by the press, who manipulated the public, which in turn, served them up as suspects.

That all changed when Detective Vincent sent Drew a text. "I got a very interesting confession out of Lizette Brown. I think you are going to want to hear this."

Drew raced out the door. On his way through his lobby, there was a messenger on his bike standing at the apartment directory. "Do you need help?" Drew quickly asked.

"Ahhh ya," he murmured. "I'm looking for a Drew? Do you know what apartment he is in?"

"Drew? I'm Drew."

"Ahhh cool. Oh, so can I see some ID?" he asked.

Drew quickly pulled out his wallet and produced his driver's license.

"Cool, here you go." He handed Drew a very thick envelop and sped off on his bike. The hefty envelop had weight to it. With hesitation, Drew unfurled the borders of the glossy casing and pulled out the pristine white and pink invitation.

Joyce White and Castro Pryorr

&

Daphne White and Katie Roma

Joyfully invite you to celebrate their double wedding in the grand ballroom of Vizcaya

Viscaya Estate and Gardens
09.24.
@ 2 o'clock in the afternoon
In the Grand Ballroom

CHAPTER 12

VIZCAYA

VIZCAYA WAS A marveled estate nestled within the city limits of Miami along beautiful Biscayne Bay. This exquisite villa exuded a timeless charm and offered a glimpse into the opulence of a bygone era. The meticulously landscaped grounds would immediately transport you to a place of grandeur and elegance.

The entrance to Vizcaya was as if you were stepping into a dream. The imposing wrought-iron gates opened up to reveal a breathtaking courtyard adorned with lush greenery, fountains, and statues. The palatial estate offered intricately designed gardens, that were both captivating and awe-inspiring.

But Vizcaya was not just a monument to wealth and beauty. It was also a cultural institution that strived to educate and inspire. The villa housed an extensive collection of European art and artifacts, showcasing the rich history and heritage of the continent. It also hosted regular exhibitions, lectures, and events that celebrated art, culture, and of course, weddings.

The car pulled in under the massive portico. Elena gracefully stepped out of the vehicle, dressed in a stunning beaded beige dress that flowed to the floor as she walked alongside Drew. Drew, sporting a sleek European cut black and white tuxedo with shiny black patent leather shoes, lowered his black and white tortoise shell sunglasses to take in their surroundings.

They entered the domed entranceway, embellished with captivating Italian Renaissance architecture, which led them towards a magnificent crystal chandelier hanging before them.

Stepping inside the villa, they meandered down the great hall admiring the meticulous craftsmanship and attention to detail that went into its construction. Every room was dressed in exquisite artwork, ornate furniture, and priceless antiques. The ceilings were adorned with stunning frescoes, and the walls were lined with tapestries and silk wallpaper. They were led to a pair of French doors, which opened up to a breathtaking tropical paradise.

As they strolled through the lush gardens, a friendly greeter from the wedding party offered them glasses of champagne. The air was filled with the delightful scent of jasmine and vibrant tropical foliage.

Elena glanced across the esplanade and spotted Israel, dressed in a crisp tuxedo, his hair wet and slicked back. He escorted Debra on one arm, who wore a soft white gown and Grace, adorned in a bright yellow dress, on his other arm.

"Don't look so nervous, Debra. It will all be alright," Elena said, kissing Debra on the cheek.

"I keep telling her that," Israel smiled. "Elena, you look stunning." They greeted each other.

"Grace, you're a vision, as always," Drew complimented as he greeted the trio.

"Well, here comes two beauties," Grace suggested as Francy and Aisha joined the group. Both were dressed in body-hugging gowns that accentuated every curve.

"This is oddly bizarre," Francy whispered. "Katie Roma told us Daphne wanted to get married."

"Well, we have a good reason to be here," Aisha hinted.

"But do we?" Debra doubted.

The dancers mingled with the effervescent crowd of uber-rich and Miami's high society.

"The press is everywhere." Debra announced as the Miami Herald stopped to photograph her. "I can just see the headline: 'Widowed fiancée haunts Vizcaya!'"

"It's high-profile," Grace chimed. "Everybody, just breathe."

The opulent ballroom, embellished with grand floor-to-ceiling windows, basked in the scorching rays of the mid-day Miami sun. The light gracefully filtered through and illuminated the resplendent golden chandeliers and exquisite Italian Renaissance paintings that seemed to glance back at them from the walls. They evoked a sense of timeless elegance.

The dancers wandered through the room in awe. "This would be an amazing space for a ballet," Debra suggested.

The luxuriously gilded wallpaper exuded a radiant luminosity, further heightening the magnificence of the makeshift altar and intricately arranged groupings of chairs. They were meticulously set to accommodate a grand gathering of a thousand esteemed guests.

"Are you with the bride or the groom's family?" An usher asked as the Sexy Seven approached.

"There's three brides," Israel wise cracked.

"The White-Roma party," Francy spoke up.

The usher quickly shuttled the group to theirs sets, midway down the aisle in the center.

An elderly woman, dressed in teal blue, put her hand on Debra's shoulder. "I'm so sorry about Ansel," she whispered.

Debra, startled from the unknown woman's advance, simply offered her a half-smile and glanced away. As Debra turned, she caught Lizette gleaming at her from the altar. Debra pretended not to see her and Lizette went on with her last-minute preparations.

"Miss Elena, you are a vision." The whole group turned to see Walter White, dressed in a creamy, off-white suit and matching tie. He reached out for Elena's hand.

"Why, Walter?" Elena obliged by extending her hand. Her diamond Tiffany bracelet, Walter's generous gift, gently slid down her wrist as he reached out and kissed it.

"I was hoping you would join me down front?" Walter pleaded. His wide-eyed, boyish charm engaged with a hint of desperation.

Elena slowly looked to Drew for an answer. He nodded his head towards the altar as Grace and Aisha stepped into the aisle so that Elena could join Walter.

That commotion caught the eye of the Spanish press, *Vistazo,* who immediately recognized Aisha from her films and came running over to the group of dancers. The crowd in the ballroom stirred. The wide-eyed society matrons started buzzing, their heads tired from turning left and right, trying to recognize every one of the who's who in the crowd.

"Aisha, Aisha! May we take your picture near the altar?" A photographer yelled out.

"But I'm not getting married, boys," Aisha snubbed.

"Your dress matches the gorgeous flowers," another complimented.

Aisha slipped on her large, round sunglasses and grabbed Francy by the arm. "If you want my picture, you will need to photograph my friend as well. Believe me, she's more famous."

Francy shot her a look as if Aisha was crazy and the frenzy of photographers jumped at the opportunity. Francy quickly slipped on her sunglasses, and the girls moved towards the altar, photographers following them like eager schoolboys.

"And then there were four," Grace commented.

Suddenly, Mendelssohn's wedding march flowed through the ballroom like a feather on the breeze. All heads turned to see Katie Roma and Castro Pryorr walking slowly down the aisle. Castro, dressed in a black tuxedo and Katie dressed in a white, more feminine version of the same tux, moved slowly down the aisle. They reached the altar and split to either side.

The room was silent. Aisha and Francy had been shuttled down to the front of the room on the opposite side the minute the wedding music started. Elena and Walter were in the front row, opposite them.

The ballroom, brimming with a multitude of esteemed guests and representatives from across the globe, found itself at maximum capacity. The assembled spectators gasped audibly as suddenly; the two radiant brides emerged into view from the opulent entrance of the ballroom.

It was a sublime sight to behold - a mother and her daughter, both exquisitely attired in artistically whimsical, matching bridal gowns, designed by no other than Wynwood's most famous atelier, Dana Posh. With an almost ethereal grace, they glided down the elegantly decorated aisle, appearing to hover above the floor.

Drew's keen eye discerned a profound serenity that engulfed Daphne's persona. He pondered whether it emanated from her union with the woman of her dreams or the fortuitous inheritance of her father's vast corporate empire she just gained. Perhaps it was both. As the women reached the ornate, floral altar, they gracefully diverged to stand beside their respective life partners.

Drew looked around the crowd. He noticed Kyle, the White's high-powered lawyer sitting close by. In the back of the room, he spotted Manford Grove. Drew knew how he warranted an invitation.

The priest raised his hand and began. "We are gathered here today to join together in marriage, Joyce White and Castro Pryorr, as well as Daphne White and Katie Roma through the vows of Holy matrimony."

Gentle music filtered through the expansive room as the couples repeated their vows. The wedding guests listened intently as the promise to love and cherish were declared by both couples.

The exchanging of rings commenced. "Should there be any valid reason for any individual to contest the union of these two couples in the sacred institution of matrimony, let them speak forthwith."

"There is."

A voice shot through the crowd like a bullet piercing the peaceful surroundings. Drew rose to his feet, commanding everyone's attention. With a purposeful clearing of his throat, he uttered the words that would send shivers down their spines, "Among us lurks a murderer."

The collective gasp that filled the room echoed with a mix of horror and curiosity. Whispers erupted like a symphony of secrets, spreading through the crowd in an instant. The entire wedding party shifted their gaze, desperate to discover the source of this disruption.

"Drew!" Katie Roma yelled. "What are you doing?"

Attempting to regain control, Drew projected his words over the commotion, each syllable dripping with suspense. "Katie, it was you who orchestrated the death of Falcon White and Ansel White, all in a desperate bid for power." Drew dropped the bomb. The weight of his revelation hung heavy in the air, swirling through the hallowed halls of Vizcaya.

Drew's gaze locked with Katie's, his eyes betraying a mix of disappointment for his friend and determination to solve the grizzly murders. The wedding attendees, now confused and enraged, struggled to make bewildered sense of the bombshell that had just been dispersed upon them. Some vehemently protested, urging Drew to retreat silently, while others wore expressions frozen in shock. "Tell me, Katie, was it all driven by greed and blackmail?" Drew pressed on, deepening the mystery that entangled them all.

Katie stood there with her mouth open. Both Joyce and Daphne White had a look of utter confusion on their faces.

"Falcon White was blackmailing you, wasn't he, Katie?" Drew asked rhetorically.

"Falcon White had proof that you were embezzling millions out of the Port of Miami, so he used that information to blackmail you."

Drew took a long breath. He could feel himself shaking inside but stayed still and calm. "When you saw no way out, you lured Falcon White under false pretenses, back to the docks for a meeting, where Castro Pryorr killed him by dropping a shipping container on him!"

The crowd responded simultaneously at the accusation. The press bolted to the altar to take pictures of the stunned wedding party.

Castro stood up, fuming with anger. "You have no proof of this lie!" He yelled out, his fists clenched in rage.

"We have complete proof, Castro. And you are going away for a very long time. The proof is all on a little flash drive that came into our possession."

Drew saw Joyce turn and look at Castro in utter disbelief.

"Katie, you told Falcon White to bring that proof on the flash drive to your meeting in exchange for incriminating information you told Falcon you had on him. Only, there was no incriminating information you had against Falcon. You used that lie to get him to the docks. Luckily, he gave that flash drive to Walter. Unbeknownst to Walter, he had no idea what was on it."

Walter was looking back and forth, unclear as to what was happening. Elena wrapped her arm around his to keep him calm.

Drew stepped out of the seats into the aisle. "You see, the flash drive had an encrypted file on it, didn't it, Israel?"

Israel quickly stood up. The room turned towards him as he addressed the crowd. "Falcon White may have been a black mailer, but he was a smart businessman. He encrypted the evidence against you, Katie. He gave the flash drive to Walter but gave the encryption key to open that file to his other son, Ansel. Isn't that right, Lizette?"

Lizette, now feeling vindicated, stood up. She shimmed her little white dress down her long legs and confirmed the truth. "Captain White gave me a series of numbers on a piece of paper to give to Ansel. I had no idea what the numbers meant at the time. I gave Ansel that paper the night he was killed."

The crowd was now so intently engrossed in the plot that you could hear a pin drop.

"The same paper that was found on Ansel's body the night he was murdered behind the nightclub, downtown. The same nightclub the Sexy Seven were performing at. Ansel was supposed to pick up his fiancée, Debra that night. But he never showed," Lizette confirmed.

Debra gasped and buried her head into Grace's shoulder. People turned to look at the unfortunate fiancée. Grace pulled her in closer to protect her.

"But you showed up that night, didn't you, Katie?" Drew confirmed. "It was at that time that Castro gave you the same knife that killed Ansel and you slipped it into my dance bag, using a handkerchief on the handle as not to get your fingerprints on the hilt."

Daphne stepped back from Katie, now in complete disbelief. "How could you?" she mumbled.

"But you didn't realize that your signature Taif Rose perfume would give you away." Drew smiled, recognizing the fact that it betrayed her several times. "Not only then, but in the car too. The morning, you attempted to rundown Debra and I on Ocean Drive during Daphne's birthday party. Your perfume lingered in the car after you attempted to make road kill out of us."

"You're crazy!" Katie screeched. "Besides, I rode with Daphne that night."

"That's why you took Lizette's car from the parking lot of the hotel that morning," Drew reveled. "The valet confirmed it was you. I'm curious, Katie? Was it just dumb luck when you happened to see us that morning on Ocean Drive and allowed your rage to run away with your common sense?"

"You took my car from the parking lot?" Lizette accused.

"Yes, she did." Elena stood up. "She left a little souvenir in the back seat." Elena pulled out of her purse, the teardrop diamond. "When you buy such expensive, one-of-a-kind pieces from Tiffanys, they have a record of which piece it is and who bought it. I noticed you have the barrettes in your hair today," Elena confirmed. Daphne turned and quickly snatched one out of Katie's hair.

"Daphne, look closely at the barrette," Elena instructed.

"It's missing a diamond!" Daphne confirmed.

"Yes, this diamond." Elena held it up for all to see, the brilliant gem catching the light. There was a collective gasp from the wedding attendees.

"That's right," Lizette recalled. "You and Daphne had just had a big fight, the night of the party. You were fighting about Debra," she pointed to the Argentinian heiress.

"I overheard that argument," Lizette continued. "Katie was upset that her rival, Debra was going to be married into the family. She stormed out of the party."

"And took off in Lizette's car," Drew added. "You should have just drove directly home, Katie."

Debra lifted her head off Grace's shoulder. She smiled with satisfaction, knowing she bested her rival. "What's that about?" Grace whispered in Debra's ear.

"It's a long story, but our long-standing scuffle was over a man. And she thought she won. It just showed me she couldn't be trusted," Debra explained.

"Wait a minute. The tension between the both of you was over a man? But I thought she was..." Grace paused.

"Fluid." Debra confirmed quickly.

"Another words, she likes debs and dudes," Grace reacted.

Now, Katie was fuming. She stepped forward to the lip of the altar. "So, I was angry," Katie snapped back. "People get angry."

"But they don't try to kill people with a car," Drew retorted. "And let's not forget about your feeble attempt at trying to get rid of the murder weapon in my bag, the night Ansel was murdered. Was that supposed to incriminate me Katie? And I thought we were friends," Drew added sarcastically. "It was a nice touch, notifying the press and accusing us of having the murder weapon."

Katie tilted her head and stared at Drew; her eyebrows furrowed.

"Allow me to walk that back for you Katie." Drew was determined. "After Castro stabbed Ansel to death in the back alley of the nightclub, he moved the body and dumped it though the hidden skylight in our dance studio at the gym. Castro was trying to send a message to us and desperately attempted to shift the blame."

Joyce White turned and slapped Castro with such force across the face that he faltered. "I can't believe you. You murderer!" She screamed. The crowd reacted.

"There were traces of coral pebbles in Ansel shoes from dragging him across the gym roof. And who knew that? Francy."

Francy stood up. "I knew that because Castro knew how to get to the roof from the street. There is a hidden door in the back alley and it's locked. When Castro and I were dating...."

Joyce White turned and slapped Castro again.

"Castro made a copy of the manager's key. We'd sneak up there and make out during our shifts. The roof has very fine white coral stones. They matched the ones found in Ansel's shoes. The police didn't know about the disguised skylights in the dance studios' roof. Only those who took class there and the gym staff knew." Francy spoke like the chairman of the board, with pride and satisfaction knowing her feelings were validated.

"What do all of you know?" Castro yelled out from the edge of the altar. "You're some dumb dancers!"

Drew calmly moved forward, closer to the altar. His undaunting attitude and peaceful disposition gave him an air of confidence. "You see, Castro, dancers are very...," he hesitated, "...astute. We can remember long sequences of movement. We see patterns, not only in rhythm and movement, but in behavior. You observe something once or twice, ok, it's an occurrence. But when you see the same behaviors and reactions over and over? It's a pattern. Humans are notorious for their patterns. You all have your patterns." Drew looked around at the crowd. "So, it's no surprise that you are all, somewhat... predictable."

You could hear a pin drop. The massive gathering of people looked at one another, surprised by the observation.

"Dancers develop a heightened sense of awareness and attention to detail. We tend to constantly analyze our own movements and the movements of those around us. This attentiveness allows us to quickly pick up on subtle changes in body language, facial expressions, and overall demeanor." Drew silenced his critics. His eyes scanned the crowd.

"Additionally, dancers excel in reading nonverbal communication. As part of our profession, we are skilled in deciphering the unspoken messages conveyed through body language, which can be critical in understanding the dynamics of a situation." He took a deep breath and walked to the center of the aisle. "By carefully observing the physicality of individuals, dancers can piece together the puzzle in a way that others might miss."

Drew turned and looked Katie straight in the eyes. "That's why you're in cahoots with Castro, because you're in love with each other," Drew concluded, pointing to Katie Roma.

Katie was speechless.

Debra rose to her feet, capturing everyone's attention. With a suspenseful pause, she began speaking directly to Katie. "You see, my dear," she whispered, her voice laced with anticipation, "who else would be willing to undertake the arduous task of covering up, hiding, and lying for him if not for you being in love? It takes a deep devotion to offer such immense sacrifices."

Debra's words hung in the air as she recounted the unforgivable deeds Castro committed in the name of love. "He killed for you. Not once, but twice," she continued...her tone, chilling. "First, Falcon White met his demise to put an end to the blackmail. And then, my fiancé Ansel's life was extinguished. Ansel told me that you tried to poach him as a business partner, but he turned you down flat." Debra smirked, knowing this would make Katie even more angry.

"So, you had him killed to satisfy your revenge against him and me. You weren't sure who had that flash drive, but assumed it was Ansel. That was your third reason for killing him." Debra's facial expression was enigmatic as she gracefully returned to her seat, leaving the room buzzing with intensity.

"You have no proof." Castro cursed.

"Oh, sufficient evidence has been obtained." Detective Vincent confidently strode through the double doors of the lavish ballroom accompanied by a squad of determined police officers.

"Castro, you cunningly manipulated the situation at the docks, operating the solitary crane you were familiar with. A crucial witness, Manford Grove, verified that you utilized his crane to drop a shipping container onto Falcon White. Although there was no concrete evidence of you checking in with security on that fateful night..." Detective Vincent paused.

With the help of his assistant, Carson, Manford Grove slowly rose to his feet so that he could look Castro in the eyes.

"The crane you manipulated required an employee ID to operate, and unwittingly, you provided it. This placed you at the scene of the crime." Detective Vincent turned to face the wedding party. "Unbeknownst to you, we discovered the small dingy you rowed across the channel in order to approach the docks discreetly, avoiding detection from the vigilant security guards." Detective Vincent slowly moved down the aisle from the doors, gesturing towards Castro.

"You knew that the only time to do this was at low tide, when large ships avoided the channel ways. Unfortunately for you, your size 13 boot print was found on the edge of the dingy you stole from the marina."

Detective Vincent paused, recounting the moment. His stance was firm and assertive.

"Furthermore, it was discovered that you lay in wait for Ansel, planning to intercept him as he came to collect Debra from the nightclub. Katie had insider knowledge that the Sexy Seven were scheduled to perform that evening, and you shadowed Ansel before ruthlessly stabbing him to death behind the club."

The priest, who was now dumbfounded by the entire list of accusations, suddenly blessed himself and darted out of the room.

"What you unknowingly failed to realize was that forensic experts uncovered traces of Ansel's blood on your favorite boots. Again, your boot print gave you away. It bears unique characteristics, accentuated by the distinct impression on your right side due to the leg fracture you suffered. Francy corroborated your accident, as did Manford Grove. He allowed us access to your work boots in his locker room. This incriminating boot impression was also discovered near a pool of blood behind the nightclub."

With a subtle nod towards Manford Grove, Detective Vincent signaled his assistant, Carson to escort Manford out of the ballroom, thanking him for his testimony with a nod.

"And let's not overlook the knife, Detective," Drew added.

Detective Vincent smiled confidently. "The blade of the knife possessed undeniable traces of Ansel's blood. However, the hilt of the blade contained minuscule traces of your own blood underneath it, Castro. It appears that in the act of thrusting the knife, you inadvertently nicked yourself," Detective Vincent expertly demonstrated. "Your prior arrest for assault and battery on an ex-girlfriend years ago, put your blood and fingerprint samples in the system. It became easy to identify you once we had the murder weapon."

Drew interjected. "And thanks to Lizette, she was the one who identified the knife as a White family heirloom. A gift from Daphne to her father. A gift she purchased in Saudi Arabia and had kept in a glass showcase in the family home."

Daphne dropped her head into her trembling hands. The thought of being betrayed by the one she loved, sickened her. She glared in Katie's direction.

Detective Vincent stepped forward. "Once we realized Falcon White was blackmailing Katie Roma, we followed the money. Falcon White had large amounts of money deposited monthly in a private account we found, thanks to Lizette. Those deposits were the blackmail money that came from Katie Roma's business account."

"So, I'm the victim here!" Katie shouted, in a poor attempt to win back her favor.

"You are no victim. You embezzled millions from the Port of Miami, premeditated two murders and two attempted murders," Drew pointed out.

The crowd reacted as if they took a gut punch to the stomach. The idea that this high-profile woman, who was in the family's inner circle, was being accused of such bloody crimes. It seemed unfathomable to most. Many of the guests turned to see the reaction of the family.

"And how was it, that Castro came to work on the docks?" Drew asked, looking in Walter's direction.

Elena gave Walter another squeeze to his arm. Walter stood up.

"I brought him into the shipping business," Walter admitted.

"How were you two acquainted?" Drew kept on Walter.

"I was an explosive expert in the Navy," Walter told the crowd. "Castro was in my regimen, working in explosives, under my supervision."

"So, Castro had knowledge of explosives, which he learned from you in the Navy?" Drew asked Walter.

Walter confirmed with a nod of his head.

"Castro, after your attempt to extinguish the White family at the cemetery, you then tried to frame Walter for the explosion. We went back to the evidence and lifted one of your fingerprints off the crudely designed bomb you rigged in the White's mausoleum," Detective Vincent confirmed. "Your poorly crafted timer went off early."

Castro paced back and forth on the altar. His face red with rage as if he was ready to explode. He was now hyperventilating with a crazed look in his eyes.

"Walter, after the explosion at the cemetery, I heard a reporter ask you about your knowledge of explosives you had from the Navy. You didn't answer the reporter but looked around in the crowd, didn't you?"

"Well, I knew it was a shot across the bow," Walter expressed, "but the only other person who was close and capable in explosives was Castro, again, trained under my own supervision."

That was the trigger that sent Castro over the edge. He turned quickly, desperate for an escape. As he did, he accidentally toppled two towering candles to the floor, causing them to collide with the elegant tablecloth draped over the nearby altar. The delicate linen instantly burst into flames, sending fiery tendrils leaping towards the heavens. In an instant, shrieks erupted from the front of the altar, filling the air with a chorus of terror. The crowd closest to the inferno quickly scattered in the opposite direction, creating a surge of panic that moved through the room like a crashing wave. Thick billows of smoke began to engulf the front of the ballroom, adding to the chaos.

Seizing the opportunity provided by the chaotic distraction, Castro darted towards the window, perceiving it as his best chance at an escape. Without hesitation, he forcefully shoved aside anyone obstructing his path, ruthlessly plowing through the human barricade. Just as he was about to reach his exit point, a powerful punch brought his scheming face into violent contact with an unyielding fist. The force of the impact jolted Castro off his feet, hurling his motionless body to the ground, surrendering him unconscious.

Standing in front of her fallen adversary, Francy poised her clenched fists like loaded rifles, prepared to strike again if needed. Yet, it only took one thoroughly satisfying blow to forcibly deconstruct this murderer from his getaway plans.

"I bet that felt good," Aisha smirked, admiring her friend.

"You have no idea," Francy replied, her smile brimming with triumph and relief.

Officers swiftly extinguished the flames as they approached the fire. The damp smell of chard debris lingered in the air. The wedding guests had evacuated, stampeding through the ballroom doors, leaving a wake of destruction behind. Now, the only ones left in the ballroom were the officers, the Sexy Seven, and the press.

They observed Detective Vincent escorting a handcuffed Katie Roma away, cursing the world for her misfortunes. Additional officers now had a conscious Castro Pryorr laced in wrist restraints, following right behind her.

Unintentionally, the press documented far more than just the wedding ceremony they had anticipated. Grace yelled out triumphantly to a group of international reporters, who were still trying to process the dramatic events, "You see, we were not the bad guys." She wagged her finger at them. "We have delivered more than you expected, haven't we?"

An intrigued reporter inquired, "Who are you people?"

After a momentary pause, Grace replied, "We are Drew and the Detectives."

At the altar, Joyce and her daughter Daphne sat side by side on small white chairs, their majestic wedding gowns intermingling. Walter joined them, offering his compassionate sympathy. The three remaining family members were mentally traumatized by the life-altering events of the past fifteen minutes.

Debra glanced towards the altar; her eyes filled with sadness. She struggled to fathom the depth of the Whites' anguish, despite her own. Regardless of one's wealth or lack thereof, the heart and mind processed trauma in a similar manner.

"And then there were three," Grace softly murmured to herself.

Israel gently rested his hand on Elena's shoulder. "How are you holding up?" he inquired, prompting a warm smile from her.

The dancers formed a close-knit circle, now surrounded by a multitude of journalists eager for a story. Questions bombarded them from all directions, but it felt as if a burden had been lifted from their weary shoulders. The arduous journey to clear their names and the unexpected predicament they found themselves in had transformed their perspective on life.

Amidst the clamor, a reporter's voice rang out above the rest, "What lies ahead for Drew and the Detectives?" The group exchanged glances, almost oblivious to the remarkable achievement they had just accomplished.

"That has a delightful ring to it," Aisha gleamed.

"Can we get a photo?" another reporter requested. Despite their exhaustion, the group of dancers rallied together, mustering their best showbiz smiles.

Drew reacted. "It's showtime, folks!"

Be sure to follow *Drew and the Detectives* as they unravel their next thrilling case through the colossal streets of New York City in *Scandal Beneath the Skyline.*

ABOUT THE AUTHOR

ANDREW PACHOLYK IS an international best-selling author who captivates his audience with masterful storytelling and intriguing characters. His award-winning work has garnered critical acclaim for intertwining life lessons, humor, and suspense with deeply humane narratives. Andrew's notable accomplishments include the prestigious Literary Titan Gold Book Award and a 2022 Ommie Award nomination for Best Spiritual Memoir for his work "Barefoot: A Surfer's View of the Universe." His creative artistry has also been featured in various prestigious media outlets including The New York Times, The Huffington Post, OM Times, and CBS News.

Connect with Andrew: https://www.peacefulmind.com/about-us

www.ingramcontent.com/pod-product-compliance
Lightning Source LLC
Chambersburg PA
CBHW052146170626
46812CB00004B/1608